When the grass wasn't greener on the other side

Sandra Hicks LaVenchi

iUniverse, Inc.
New York   Bloomington

When the grass wasn't greener on the other side

iUniverse books may be ordered through booksellers or by contacting:

iUniverse
1663 Liberty Drive
Bloomington, IN 47403
www.iuniverse.com
1-800-Authors (1-800-288-4677)

ISBN: 978-1-4401-3632-0 (pbk)
ISBN: 978-1-4401-3633-7 (ebk)

Printed in the United States of America

iUniverse rev. date: 4/28/2009

ACKNOWLEDGEMENT

I would like to first give thanks to GOD who has given me wisdom, knowledge and understanding to write and deliver my talents. To my daughters, who encouraged me to go against the odds. To Mrs .Teresa Bingley, who helped to mold me into the woman I am today. To Captain Dan and Marie Jones, who gave me unconditioner love and guided me. To Terry Walsh, who supported my dreams.

To my mother, Jessie and my father, Jimmy; To my pastor, Dr. Creflo Dollar, who sermons taught me to never stop dreaming. To Horace Christian and I also would like to thank those who believed in me… you pushed me and those who didn't believe in me... you pushed me.

Special Thanks to:

Denver and Paige

CHAPTER 1
GIRL YOU NEED A CHANGE... TRY A THUG!

It was a cold November night and things in my house were what some people would call abnormal, which was my normal home life. The kids were running around the house playing while I was closed up in the bedroom talking on the phone to my cousin, Vanessa and our girlfriend Belinda. At the same time my drug addictive husband Tony was beating on the bedroom door begging me for ten dollars to get a bag of weed.

"Seneca open this damn door! I already told you that this was the last time. Now you're pissing me off, so you need to give me the money!" Tony whined with rage.

I tried to ignore him and continue my conversation on the phone, but with all the beating and yelling Tony was doing it was nearly impossible. From time to time he would get quiet, then after a few minutes he would start back up and beating and yelling louder than before. It was going on the second hour of his rambunctious ass behavior and Tony was not giving up. He took it up to the next level and began picking the lock on the door trying to get in. I looked towards the door and thought that if he got the door open and came in starting some shit with me, that I was going to bust his fucking head open with my phone. "Tony, you need to go on about your business now. I've already told you no!" I screamed repeatedly as I jumped off of the bed with my cellphone still to my ear. I quickly told my girls to hold on, and I grabbed a chair and wedged it underneath the doorknob to make it harder for him to get in. They could still hear me murmuring.

"Seneca, Seneca," Vanessa called out my name several times to get my attention, but although I had the phone up to my ear I couldn't hear exactly what she was trying to say because I was focused on securing the door.

"That motherfucker will have a hard time getting in here," I said out loud and checked to make sure the door was in fact secured.

"Are you back on the phone?" Belinda asked in a sarcastic tone. Before I could answer Belinda, Vanessa said, "Girllll...I don't know why in the hell you're locking yourself up in a room, you know you gotta come out at sometime or another. So, you might as well open the door."

"Sheeed, you got that right!" Belinda agreed. "You know his ass is going to be posted there all night or worse than that you might decide to come out and your car is fucking gone."

They both laughed as I thought silently for a second. She's probably right I better open the door. So without hesitation, I jumped up and sprinted to open the door. I removed the chair and turned the knob to open the door. Tony stood there in his not-yet changed work clothes that he wore to cut grass in and dirt and grass plunging off of him. I frowned and turned up my nose. I turned around and got back on my bed. He asked me who I was talking to. Not responding to his question, I sat down and went back to talking to the girls.

"Girl, I know that's right. For real, I did that shit too. It was the bomb."

Vanessa started asking me what the fuck I was talking about when Belinda interrupted, "Now Vanessa I know you know what time it is. All the times you were flexing on the phone talking to me and pretending that we were talking about some good shit, when your man comes walking into the room, and you know he's was trying to listen to your conversation." "Damn, my bad Sen., I thought you were tripping or something" Vanessa said laughing.

"Girl, we'll never get you mixed up with Flow Jo, your ass is Slow Jo," Belinda cried. I cleared my throat to keep from laughing out loud at what Belinda had said, and then I got up and walked into my bathroom to look in the mirror. I noticed that Tony was following me. I could smell the stench of dirt and sweat behind me surfing right up my nose.

"Give me the ten dollars, Seneca. I gave you all my damn money to put up and all I want is ten dollars."

I turned around immediately and yelled, "Hell no! Your ass didn't give me anything. I had to sit there and take it and if I hadn't been there to get the money when you cashed the check, every crack head and drug dealer in Atlanta would be banking our bill money right now! Now, you need to go take your ass a bath and get up this grass you don drop on my carpet!" I screamed at the top of my lungs. I could hear the girls on the phone laughing their ass off, but I didn't want to say anything to them until after he left the room. I stormed out of the bathroom and he was right on my ass. He seemed to have paid no attention to what I said because he continued begging. This was a tactic he used often, because he knew if he just kept right on begging that I would give in. Looking at me with intense, bloodshot eyes Tony said, "Look Seneca, Give me ten dollars and I'll be right back. You got my word this is the last time."

I looked up at him with anger, despair and sadness in my eyes and once again said, "No, No, No! We ain't going through this shit again tonight! Every day and night it's the same old bullshit and I'm tired of it. You need to get some help!"

Tony became extremely aggravated when I said that and told me that he didn't need any help for weed because people don't get hooked on it. He reminded me that he was a grown ass man who didn't need me telling him what to do. Tony's so-called non-addictive weed habit had become an everyday thing that was keeping him high and me mad as hell. You need to try smoking weed and maybe it would make you more relaxed, Tony would always say, but I wasn't about to try something that gave you a false sense of security. Besides, I looked at Tony as the weakest link and as for me, doing drugs was not an option. Belinda and Vanessa kept pressing the buttons on their phones to make that bleeping sound to get my attention.

Tony heard the noise and looked at the cellphone and said in an inquisitive tone, "You still on the fucking phone while I'm talking to you? Mannnn… you ain't even right! You're trying to embarrass me in front of those bitches. I'm your fucking husband!" Tony yelled and stormed out the room. He continued yelling that he was going to go pawn our TV if I didn't give him the money. I knew he wasn't going to do it, because he knew he would be up shit creek with me, so I paid him no mind and proceeded to return to my conversation as he continued to spew out threats. I had been with Tony for sixteen years and it was pretty much all I knew. In fact, I didn't even know much about me. I didn't have much time to find myself because I was pregnant at sixteen and had this grown ass man wanting to take care of me by showering me with gifts and money. Needless to say, he was a drug dealer who thought buying me meant that he could control me. He became abusive both physically and emotionally. Tony smoking eventually led to other drug abuse. He seemed to be getting more desperate for it by the day, and could never get enough. Tony had this problem way before I came into the picture. He was an ex-addict, who had recovered and was starting a new life. At that time, I didn't know much about drugs. I was naïve and gullible and didn't care about his past. I was focused on all the money and gifts he was buying my little girl and I. Over time I began to realize that I was trapped in a dangerous situation. Tony went to prison four or five times for selling drugs, but he always made sure I was taking care of. So I didn't leave him because I thought that he was in love with me, but nevertheless, he was really in control of me. So had it not been for me controlling the money we would have ended up broke, busted and disgusted long time ago. I didn't like weed and thought it was for people who couldn't handle the cards that life was dealing them, so they looked for the easiest possible way to escape their agony. I always knew Tony would take dope to the next level; it was just a matter of time. It's not like I could have stopped him, he was at the point of no return. He would maneuver the whole situation and raise hell to just to get high. Let me put it another way, if he wasn't high nobody in whole damn neighborhood was going to be happy. His drug problem had become more of a disorder than a habit. Sometimes he would fiend so hard I would tell him Nigga, go smoke a tree or something. Anything, I don't give a flying fluke of a fuck! One time he was fiending so I told him to eat a spider and I would give him ten dollars. I was only kidding, but to my surprise he found a spider in the crack of a porch and pulled that spider from the web by one of its' many legs and put it in his mouth! I screamed and said, "Tony, are you fucking crazy! How the hell could you do that?"

He gave me a grave look and said, "Now give me my ten dollars."

It was then that I realized there was some serious shit going on with him. I gave him the money and he left for the Westside to get in weed. I thought to myself, Yeah right … weed! That spider shit did not seem like the work of a weed head. But what did I know; I've never done drugs so I wouldn't consider myself an expert. Some of my religious friends used to say that it didn't seem like I gave a damn about him, but truth be told … I somewhat did. I became wrapped up in the sickness of his problems and still trying to manage a job, my home and family. I was young and had high aspirations of becoming a model and actress, but growing old in my spirit all because I'd made a bad decision to grow up fast and take on such a great responsibility as a young girl.

When I put the phone back up to my ear; I could hear them ranting and raging about my situation and laughing all in the same breath. Clearing my voice, I could hear that they got quiet. "Y'all finished?" I asked.

Belinda started back laughing because everything was so funny to her. I was beginning to getting upset with her, because Tony had my nerves in an uproar and I was trying to talk to them all at the same time. Belinda was cool, but she really could care less about the issue because she didn't have a man in her life, so she wasn't putting up with the bullshit that I endured. She possessed a "don't give a dam attitude" about men and I believe she wanted to impose her views upon Vanessa and I because she felt she knew more about fucked up relationships with men, due to the fact that she had been there and done that. I'd still say that she couldn't relate to my circumstances, unlike Vanessa. Vanessa, who I called her Nessa for short, could relate more to what I was going through because like Tony her husband, Robert was on heavy drugs too. Belinda didn't give me time to explain anything before she quickly ranted off saying, "Seneca, enough of this bullshit girl! You are way too beautiful and smart to keep going through that dumb shit with him. I mean … I know that's your husband and all, but girl you need a change. Seneca you got to at least try a thug!"

I listened quietly to her go on and on; I agreed secretly that she was at least 80 percent right. Belinda's preferred men were were thugs and she said that they fucked better, sucked better and that every woman needed a thug in her life. She scared the hell out of me, 'cause I understood that a thug was the bomb in bed and would have your pussy everyday. I was laughing but very intrigued by her explicit descriptions. "Damn, girl you make it sound like a thug would have you sprung for life," I muttered, trying to not talk loud because I didn't want Tony to hear me.

Belinda turned on her radio in the background and she started singing the rap song, "Make the pussy pop, drop it like it's hot-hot," she sanged loudly. "Man, I'm telling you Seneca, a thug would have you singing rap, reggae and R&B all at the same time cause that dick be soooo good!" Belinda screamed over the music. She then turned the music down and waited for me to respond.

I thought about everything she was saying and said, "Sheeed, It's not like I'm fucking Tony anyway. All he does is cut grass, get high and cook Pinto beans and cornbread all the fucking time anyway." They started laughing, and then I told them that I wouldn't mind hanging out with them and besides, Belinda made it sound so good. Vanessa suggested that we all get together that night and go to Club Mirage to see the male strip show and also start the mission of finding me a bone-hard thug. "Let's meet up at my house" Vanessa suggested and we all agreed. I didn't mind going out to the club because the Mirage was the place to be on a Saturday night, but I wasn't too keen on meeting a thug. All my life, I've always dealt with the clean cut, muscled, well built guys. I knew that night it would be a problem getting out because not only was Tony not high, he was also insecure and jealous and couldn't stand to see me out having a good time with girls he couldn't stand. That's why I stopped going out; I didn't want him cussing out my friends and fighting with them. You see, I would have never even thought about dealing with a man with braids, gold teeth or who wore pants hanging down his ass. I would see guys like that and turn my nose up at them, strongly thinking to myself, that nigga is shot out. I knew I wanted to go, but only one thing was holding me back from going, or should I say making it hard for me to get out the house. The very thing I hated doing was the one thing that was going to set me free that night to hang out with the girls. All the other times I gave him money for dope was because he made the house unbearable to live in with his whining and outbursts of rage when he didn't get his way. But this time, I wanted something and a trade off seemed bearable at the time. I told the girls that I was going to hang out with them, but I needed to call them back.

"Girl, don't change your mind and stay home being miserable with Tony now!" Belinda said before hanging up. I assured them that I was going out and then we hung up.   As I walked to the living room I didn't see Tony anywhere in sight. I ran towards the front door to check if my car was still in the driveway, when I heard some rattling in the den. With a worried, curious look on my face, I walked swiftly into the den to see what was going on. The lights were off and Tony was looking through my drawers and underneath the sofa for some change to get up to buy his weed. I flicked on the light and he looked up and noticed me watching him, then he stop and asked me if I was going to give him the money. I walked towards the mess that he had made in the den and stopped to pick up some important papers that he had scattered all over the floor. I looked at him and told him that he had a serious problem and needed to get some help, but for right now I would give the ten dollars, if he let me go out with my girls. Without hesitation he agreed to it, just like I thought. I went to the bedroom to get my purse and gave him the ten dollars and then he said that he would be back in about forty-five minutes.

I was excited, yet skeptical about going out because he had to look after the kids while I was gone. I started giving myself a talk so that I wouldn't change my mind. He always keeps the kids when I'm at work and nothing happens to them. Besides, those are his kids too. He's gotten high before and always seems to manage well. I kept telling myself these things and more as I looked in on my kids playing in their room, and then I went to my room to get dressed.

I looked through my closet, trying to find something sexy and but sophisticated to wear. I came across a black and white tight fitting shirt with a black tie and black pants. After taking a shower and getting dressed, I called Vanessa and Belinda and told them that I was dressed and was waiting for Tony to come back from the store.

"Whaddd… I can't believe you're really going!" Belinda cried.

"Now how the hell did you pull that one off?" Vanessa asked.

I told them that it wasn't easy. We sat on the phone talking about the club and what they'd heard Tony and I arguing about. About thirty minutes later Tony pulled back into the driveway. "Okay, he's here y'all. It's 8:15 and I'm getting ready to leave the house" I continued.

"Hurry up the male review starts at 9:30," Belinda shouted.

By that time, Tony was in the house walking towards the bedroom smiling, with two fifty cent blunts in his hands. He seemed much calmer and he barely even noticed the skintight outfit I was wearing. I believed he didn't care because he had just gone to pick up lady package to keep him company and she was dressed all in white, or maybe it was green. I went into the kid's room and kissed them goodnight; then yelled out to him that I was leaving and on my way to Decatur. Tony didn't utter a word back at me. He was now content with his drug of choice. As I looked back, I could see him licking a blunt and preparing to fill it with dope. I shook my head and headed to meet up at Vanessa's place.

CHAPTER 2
MEET ME AT THE CLUB

I arrived at Vanessa house at five minutes to nine and Belinda was already there. When I pulled up to the door and parked they were standing outside talking; Vanessa was smoking a cigarette. They had on their regular get-up gear on Nessa wore black legging and a body shirt with a big belt and Belinda had on jeans and a halter top that showed off her mid-section. When I got out of my car they both said, "Uhh ... shit! Look at Senecaaaa ... looking all sexy and ready for her thug."

I shook my head and smirked," Ya'll are crazy as hell!" We all laughed and set out for Club Mirage, arriving at 9:15. The club was jumping as usual. When we walked in everyone was around the stage getting ready to watch the male review show. We found a table and sat down to watch the male strippers do their thing and the ladies dish out their dollars. One of the strippers made his way around to our table. "Seneca, give me two dollars," Vanessa said, holding her hand out and acting like she was about to lose her damn mind.

"Girl, I'm going to watch but I'm not about to give those niggas' in g-strings my loop. They need to be paying me to come watch them." I said sarcastically.

Vanessa stood up, patting her pockets and looking for a dollar to give to the stripper. I looked up and noticed that Vanessa was still searching, so I ended up handing her a dollar just so she could be happy. It's not that she didn't have any money; she just didn't want to spend it. She quickly snatched the dollar bill out of my hand and laid it on the strippers' sweaty hard stomach, looking directly at his package. Pulling on her arm, I yelled "Nessa, Nessa! Girl you act like you're about to suck his dick. You're so close up on it." She laughed it off and kept on watching. In fact, I don't think she even heard me because she didn't snap.

After the strip show was over Belinda, got on the dance floor to dance, or should I say, take over. What I mean is every time she got up to dance the women in the club would literally clear the floor because she intimidated them. Belinda was a stripper as well, but she also loved the attention she got when she danced.

Vanessa was quiet and shy, sneaky, undercover freak. She always pretended to be broke and when guys came up and offered to buy me a drink, she would stand behind my back whispering in my ear, "Get the drink for me." This was our usual routine since I didn't drink and besides, she was my cousin who cried broke every time we hung out. But I didn't mind looking out for her like that because she was my road dog, my secret soldier that I told everything too.

I had to go to the bathroom not to use it, but to check out the men who sat at the bar near the ladies room. I started making my way there and before it could pass the bar this very tall, dark, suspect of a thug with long braids approached me. "Hey Lil Kim," he said smiling down at me.

I stopped dead in my tracks and said with an attitude," Uh… My name is not Lil Kim. My name is Seneca." Still smiling down at me, he then apologized and introduced himself, "I'm Derron."

I shook his hand and briefly carried on small talk with him, and then I excused myself and continued making my way to the ladies room. I made it to the washroom and hung out for about five minutes, talking and prancing in the mirror. As I walked back to my seat I suddenly thought about the guy I had just met and pondered, could I consider him a thug? Halfway to my seat I paused again to analyze and answer that question. I visualized his features. Well…let's see, now he has long braids, and he does have a gold tooth, but, but…. His pants aren't hanging off of his ass. Now I'm confused! I was wondering if he had to have all three attributes to qualify him as a true thug. I presumed that two out three wasn't bad, but I wasn't sure so I decided to ask Belinda. When I looked for her on the dance floor she was almost up on the ceiling, doing one of her spider woman moves. I smirked and shook my head. After seeing that, I knew I had to wait to ask her. I'm very analytical so I wanted to make sure that I had truly met a thug.

Once I arrived back at my seat, I did not mention the guy to Vanessa at all. We just watched the male strippers, laughed, drank virgin and non-virgin cocktails and got our party on. After about fifteen minutes, someone suddenly tapped me on my shoulder and when I turned around, to my surprise, it was him "the Almost Thug" I had met on my way to the ladies room. I looked up at him and so did Vanessa. Vanessa whispered in my ear and said, "Oooowe... Now that's a thug.

Biting my bottom lip, I responded, "Are you serious?" Vanessa looked over her Prada glasses and said, "Let me put it this way. If you don't jump on it, one of these hoodrats will." Then she turned back around towards the dance floor and started dancing in her seat. I laughed and looked back up at him. "Ms. Lady, I've been looking for you," he said, bending down.

"Well obviously, you was looking damn hard, 'cause you found me," I said in a sassy tone. I got to admit I loved his relentless determination, so I offer him a seat to see what type of suave he had about himself. As he sat down, he gave me a napkin with his number on it.

"Here's my number. Make sure you use it," he whispered in my ear. "Can I buy you a drink?" he continued.

I then told him that I didn't drink alcohol and before I could finish my sentence he interrupted, "That's some good shit dare. I like women who don't drink. You know somebody got to be sober, right?" he chuckled. As we continued to talk, I played with the napkin on the table in front of me and decided to put in my purse later. "Well I don't drink, but you can buy my cousin a drink if you like." I muttered. His reaction to what I said was kind-of honestly foul.

He replied," I usually don't buy women drinks, and I offered you the drink; but since she's your cousin I'll go ahead and do it."

I sat there quiet for a second smiling because I didn't know what to say after that. I turned to Vanessa and asked her what she wanted to drink. She was grinning ear to ear and told me that she wanted a Long Island Iced Tea. "Good looking out cuz," she whispered in my ear over the loud music. I shook my head and turned around to continue talking to Derron. Derron got the waitress' attention and she came over.

"What does your cousin want to drink?" he asked as he gave the waitress the order.

"Oh, she just wants a Long Island... that's all."

Derron had a clammy look on his face as if he couldn't believe he was doing it. I put my hand on his shoulder and thanked him for buying the drink. Shortly, the waitress brought over his Corona and Vanessa's Long Island; then Vanessa turned her attention elsewhere because she was getting her drink on. After taking care of the waitress, Derron turned his attention back towards me. "Now back to you," he said as he pulled my stool closer to him. "What did you say your name was again?"

"It's Seneca," I replied, trying to talk more in his ear. Derron started smirking and said, "Isn't that the name of some damn Apple juice or something?" I gave him a hard stare, then I smirked and said, "Very funny, but since you're a comedian I'll let you entertain me a little while." Derron put in long arm over my shoulder. "I'm sorry. I was just kidding with you, but I bet you're as sweet as apple juice; if not sweeter," he murmured looking me straight in my eyes. He had the most beautiful big eyes that I had ever seen. He reminded me of Omar Epps in that movie *Juice*. I smiled at him and then bashfully looked away. He gently put his hand on my chin and lifted my face towards his. "You're very beautiful. Are you married?" Okay, time to go, he asking me about my marriage.

I looked up at him and slowly said, "Yes, I am married, but … " Derron interrupted and said, "Thank you for being honest. See that's what I'm talking about; I like fucking with a grown ass woman, cause most of these girls be on some little girl shit." His response was surprising because he didn't care about me being married. I didn't know how to respond, so for the next three hours I just listened to him talk about himself and how he liked my style. We were totally into each other's conversation, style, movement, eye contact, body chemistry and everything else. Without my permission he started kissing me on my neck so passionately, moving his long, wet tongue up and down the side of my neck. Although I never been the One-Night Stand type of female, it seemed like the right time to try it out, because he was making love to me mentally and I was loving every minute of it. I felt a breeze in between my legs and I noticed that my panties were wet. The cool air from the air conditioner made me realize that I had came a little from all the foreplay. The night grew short and the morning hours were just around the corner. The room was quieter and all I could hear was my heart beating every second and the depth of my breathing because we were so zoned out and into each other and weren't acknowledging the crowd or the music around us. Not grasping the fact the club was closing, we sat there with never ending stories to tell each other.

Vanessa tapped me on my shoulder and told me that the club was getting ready to close. He looked down at the time on my his cellphone and said, "Yeah, it's four in the morning." I thought about my makeup and hair. It must be a complete mess by now. I had not touched up in four hours. "I'll be right back Derron. I'm going to the restroom," I excused myself. As he was finishing the last of his Corona he whispered, "I'll be waiting right here when you get back." When I got up to leave he reached out and rubbed my ass. I didn't care because it felt good and I wanted to be a half-bad girl that night after meeting him. I must have stay in the ladies room for about twenty minutes or more because my panties were so wet from all the foreplay that I had to take them off to try to dry them. I sat on the toilet thinking about how Tony was going to act when I got home; then I thought about Derron and instantly didn't give a fuck how Tony was going to act.

I finished up in the restroom and rushed out back to him, but when I got back to the table where I left him he was gone. "Wh-where did he go?" I muttered as I looked around in confusion. Where is Nessa? And where is Be- but when I looked towards the dance floor I saw Belinda was still dancing and Vanessa was wandering around the club looking lost. "What the hell is going on?" I exclaimed in a low tone. I went over to Vanessa and she was in the corner looking on the floor searching for something. She said in a slurred voice, "Girl, I don lost my keys." I looked at her squirming face and tried to help look for her keys, but I couldn't help wondering about Derron and trying to figure out why he would just leave without saying goodbye. Then I remembered that he gave me his number on a napkin, so I ran back to the table we were sitting only to find that the waitress was getting ready to clean up. I yelled out to her," Wait!" in a panicking voice. She looked at me like I was crazy as hell and said, "For what!" as she continued putting beer bottles and cups in the black plastic bag. "Umm … I- I seemed to have left something and this is the table where I was sitting. Could you give me two minutes to check?" I replied in a humble, but desperate voice. She chuckled and told me that if it's some money, I might as well charge it to the game because I wouldn't find it. She then told me she'd give me a few minutes to look and walked to clean another table. I scrambled through all the paper and napkins in hopes to finding the napkin he wrote his number on. The napkin was nowhere to be found. I looked over at the waitress and yelled out to her asking her if she wouldn't mind me looking through the bag of trash that she had. "Sheeed, honey I got to go home to my kids," she replied.

I guess I might as well forget about it I said as I began to walk away. While walking back towards Vanessa, I looked back once more toward the table thinking about the great time I had with Derron and how I would never get a chance to know him. I couldn't bear the thought of giving up so easily on something I really wanted, so I walked back over to the table and looked underneath it. Lying under the chair was a half soaked napkin with a shoe print on it. I carefully picked it up so I wouldn't rip it and slowly unfolded it and to my surprise it was the napkin with his number.

"Cuz, me boo. You gotta move 'cause I got to finish up over here. Ain't got time for you to keep looking for something you ain't gonna find anyway," the waitress said as she started gathering the rest of the trash off of the table as I was stooped down under it. "My balls, Sweetie, I'm done anyway." I sighed. The waitress looked at me with her faced puffed up and said,"What tha hell you mean your balls?! If you got balls then you really got your issues." I became offended but then I realized that when everyone else says "My Bad" and I always say "My Balls." People always give me the same response when they hear me say that. I didn't have time to explain that to her, so I told her thanks and then I got out of her way. I rushed to the bathroom to dry the napkin so I wouldn't smear the ink. As I was running towards the bathroom, Belinda had got off of the dance floor and was helping Vanessa. "Seneca, girl, come help us find these keys," Belinda yelled across the room. I threw my hand up and told them that I'd be right back to help. In the bathroom, I held the napkin up to the hand-dryer for a good thirty seconds. When I looked at it afterwards, I could see the phone number a lot better. It was smeared a bit, but I could make out what it was. I placed the napkin into my purse and went out to help search for the keys.

By that time, the manager had turned on all the lights in the club. The club manager came up to us and said, "You ladies got to leave now, but you can return in the afternoon to search for the keys. Vanessa said in an indistinct voice, "We can't leave because my car key is on that ring." The manager gave us a nonchalant shrug and told us again to leave the club.

So the three of us stood in front of the club trying to figure out what we were going to do. As we stood there, thoughts of the 6 foot 7 thug danced through my mind. Vanessa needed to go to her grandmother's house to get her extra set of keys and I could have taken her, but I wanted to use that as an excuse to call Derron. So I took out the napkin and called his number. The phone rang and rang then a deep, easygoing voice said, "Hello." For a quick second, I paused; I then said, "Derron? This is Seneca. The one you met tonight in the club." His voice lit up as if he was happy to hear from me. "What's up? What happen to you?" he gathered in a keyed up voice. "I waited at the table for you for about twenty-five minutes." He continued.

"Well... I was in the restroom and when I came out you were gone," I responded. Belinda and Vanessa nudged me and whispered, "Ask him to come get us." I moved further away from them so I could talk in private and then looked back at them and inaudibly mouthed, "Wait, Wait!"

Derron was talking but I missed what he was saying because of them, so I interrupted him in the middle of the conversation and asked him if he didn't mind, could he do me a favor? Derron was sound a bit skeptical, but eager at the same time. Maybe he thought I was going to ask him to do another favor for my cousin. Actually, it was another favor for her. "Uhh... what is it?" he said slowly. I went on to explain that Vanessa lost her keys in the club and that we were stranded and asked him if he could come back and give us a ride. "Well, I was almost home, but I'll turn around and be there in about ten minutes," he said. I told the girls that he was coming back to help us and then we all huddled up in a corner to keep the cold wind off us. Seconds later, a long, cream colored Cadillac pulled up to the door. I didn't know what he was driving so I looked carefully before leaping. He then rolled down the passenger-side window and motioned for us to come on in.

Just before we jumped in the car I thanked him for the ride. Vanessa and Belinda jumped in the backseat as I pulled the seat latch to let them get in. "Where do you need to go?" Derron asked Vanessa looking over his shoulder. Vanessa was out of it from drinking too much, so I answered. "She's going to her grandma's house down the street to get her extra set of keys. I'll show you how to get there." Derron nodded his head and took the directions as I gave them. After getting the keys, we arrived back at the club around five in the morning. The girls thanked him and then went to their car to head home. "You can park right next to my car in the back of the club," I said as I looked over at him.

"Car? You mean to tell me you have a car and you needed me to take Vanessa to get her keys?" he emphasized. I looked a little timid at first until he smiled and shook his head. "Well yeah, but I wanted to-" But before I could finish my sentence he started laughing and said, "It's cool, I know what you did and I'm glad you did it." Derron parked near my car in the back. "Why don't you come and sit in my lap?" he whispered; frost came from his mouth as he spoke. I didn't say a word, just got up and spread my legs across his lap. What awaited me was his massive, hard dick. My panties got extremely wet again, but I maintained control over myself because I really liked this guy and I wanted him to respect me. He saw the expression on my face; then asked me if I wanted to see it. I looked away bashfully and turned back to him and said, "No, I can wait."

We started kissing and grinding until the windows were completely fogged and before I knew it, the sun was getting ready to rise. I somehow peeled my lips away from his lips and moaned, "I got to go now." I didn't want to leave, but I had to. Derron ignored my plea for release and stuck his tongue down my throat. He started sucking my lips and probing my ass with no signs of quitting. I knew Tony would probably be up waiting for me to start some shit about me staying out all night and we would more than likely end up fighting. The funny thing is that I didn't care; I had such an interest in this new found thug that Tony was not going to affect me with anything he said or did. Even in such a short period of time, I felt that this guy was going to be worth it in the end. Derron finally came to a halt and released me from his long, strong arms. We kissed for the last time that morning and I peeled myself out of his arms and got in my car to head home.

CHAPTER 3
TOO GOOD TO BE TRUE

Driving down I-285 with the window down and wind blowing on my face to keep me awake, I knew that Tony's weed high must have worn off by now. Shit, he is going to be pissed off as hell about me coming in so late. The whole ride home, my mind was focused on that bona fide thug that seduced me, yet I couldn't help but remember what I was getting ready to go home to. I had startling thoughts about how Tony would beat on me, rape and hold me hostage in my own house. In the past Tony had been very abusive, physically and mentally, but since I've became a woman I put the brakes on that shit. I began fighting back and cutting his ass everyway but lose. I became a bulldog even though when all alone, I was really a poodle. I never had to fight anyone and now I was fighting almost every day to survive. I became the bitch I needed to be, to deal with a bitch-boy, a coward and a junkie. I always knew I should leave, but I didn't know how.

It seemed like a long ride home because I was so sleepy and couldn't stay awake. Fifteen minutes later, I pulled into the driveway of my house and my heartbeat became rapid. I turned off my cellphone and put it in my purse. All I kept thinking about was this thug called Derron and how I was anxious to see him again. When I walked into the house everyone except Tony was still asleep, but strangely, Tony was very calm and quiet, which only meant one thing. He was fucked up from the neck up. He must have gotten up and smoked before I got home; that's the only way he would have been so composed. I walked past him on the sofa where he was sitting and smiled. As I went by him he said, "Did you have a good time?" in a sarcastic voice.

I responded, "I'll let you figure that out," then I went to bed and slept until about two in the afternoon. I didn't go to church, Sunday school or to any religious places back then because my life was so abnormal and crazy that I could I never find the time. Besides, my spirit wasn't right and I was in anguish most of the time in this relationship with Tony.

When I woke up that afternoon, the kids were in the yard playing and Tony was in the living room watching football. I got my phone out of my purse and turned it on to check my voicemail. I was eager to see if Derron had called, so I proceeded to check my messages with one ear on the phone and the other one listening out for the footsteps of my husband. My heart quivered and the keenness of waiting for the voicemail to play made me anxious. First, I had to look around to make should Tony wasn't around the corner spying, and then I pressed one on the phone to listen to my messages. Derron had left a message expressing how cute I sounded on my voicemail message, and that he would like to take me to lunch or dinner. I called him back later and we talked about my marriage, his singleness, my kids, his kids and everything else under the sun. I was really expressive with him because he was different, first of all he was very articulate, humorous, intelligent and yes it was official ... he was a thug! This guy amazed me with his familiarity and versatility in different subjects. Making love to my mind was the most ultimate test of all and he passed. I was hooked mentally, but he hadn't yet pulled me in physically. Derron made love to my mind in ways that were challenging, refreshing, and left me wanting to get to know more of him.

Every conversation after that was filled with laughter, joy, and sexual enticement. Although we wanted to be with each other, he understood that I was married with children and that I had to be careful about moving too fast.

One week before Thanksgiving, Derron was leaving to go to his hometown of Kentucky to be with his family. We talked or texted each other every day until he arrived there, and during the course of his stay in Kentucky he would still call me every day, expressing how much he wanted to see me. He was really showing me that he wanted me as his girl, his woman and lady.

CHAPTER 4
ENTICEMENT

One week later, Derron came back to Atlanta and the girls and I got together with him and we all decided to go out to another club. We met at his house, but since I was riding with the girls I decided to stay with them. He wanted me to ride with him, but my theory has always been that if we come together, we leave together. We followed Derron to a club called Twenty Grand East and when we arrived, Derron and I walked around the club holding hands. Belinda started doing her thing on the dance floor and Vanessa got a drink with Derron's cousin, Ernest, and sat down. Derron and I took pictures together, and he really seemed to be into me ... just me. He kissed me constantly and told me how beautiful I was. I felt alive again, as if this was all meant to happen. This guy had really breathed life back into me again. I felt feelings I hadn't felt in the twelve years or more since I'd been with Tony.

We sat down at a table and ordered hot wings, chicken fingers and fries. He did most of the eating. I watched him eat because I guess I was so wrapped in his looks and charm that I wasn't hungry...at least for food anyway. When Derron finished his food he looked over at me and said, "Now back to you baby." I laughed and just gazed into his big brown eyes. I felt his hand on my leg under the table, and then he went between my legs and moved on up to my panties ... Oh wait, this time I wasn't wearing any. He guided his long thick finger into my well-kept, wet pussy. I was paralyzed and I couldn't move; it was like I was spellbound or something. I stared directly at him and did not move at all, though I continued spreading my legs further apart underneath the table. I bit my bottom lip trying very hard not to moan, but the feeling of his thick finger sliding in and out of me almost bought me to tears. I began motioning my hips around discreetly giving him back more of what he was giving me. "Seneca, Seneca... ...don't move," he whispered. "Keep looking at me ... Yeah, that's it, that's it," he continued in a low deep voice. He leaned over as if he was going to kiss me, then he pulled back. He repeated this several times as if he knew exactly what he was doing, knowing that I wanted him to tongue me right about ... yester-year!

By the end of this date, I was wearing fuck-fo-culars and had been mentally made love to again, just in depth this time. Later on in the evening, or morning, we all left the club and I went home, but Vanessa and Belinda went to an after-hours spot while Derron and his cousin went back to his place. I had no choice but to leave, but he begged me to stay with him. I just didn't see that happening so soon, being as we had just recently met and I truly was not ready to give my goodies up to him.

Tony was at home baby sitting, and this continued because after Derron called to order my attention, my time and my mind, I actually started giving Tony dope money daily just so I could get out of the house to be with Derron. I arrived home around about three in the morning and when I came in the door the kids were asleep and Tony was nowhere to be found. I woke up my oldest daughter and asked her if Tony left. "I don't know, Mommy," she said and went back to sleep.

I walked into the kitchen to get something to drink and heard a movement from underneath the kitchen table. It scared me, but I stooped down to look under the table and saw Tony high as hell sitting under there trying to catch me into something. "What the hell? What the hell are you doing?!" I yelled in a curious, but frightened voice. He didn't answer me, then got up and asked me, where have I you been?

I looked at him with rage in my eyes and walked away. I went into my bedroom and started taking off my jewelry and shoes. Tony walked behind me asking the same question over and over. I finally said that I had been out to the club and that I didn't ask what choice drug he going to use on certain days. Tony kept staring at me and biting his lip as if he was getting ready to hit me. I picked up a shoe over my head just in case he wanted to try something. "Yeah, one of these days I'm going to catch you with your boyfriend," he said and walked out of the room. I didn't even respond and when I knew he was out of sight I closed my door and took off my clothes to go to sleep.

After about twenty minutes of lying there almost asleep I heard something making a sniffing sound in the dark. I opened my eyes and Tony was standing with his head bent down towards lower part of my body. I instantly sat up and said to him, "What the hell are you doing, you crazy ass man?" He raised his head up and asked me to allow him to smell my pussy. "Let you smell... my what? You better take your high ass out of here," I screamed. He stared at me with his eyes redder than a fire engine and walked out of the room and didn't return.

The next morning I got up to go to the store, but I really wanted to leave so I could talk to Derron. I called him and asked him if I could come over, and he said yes. So when that evening after I came home from work, I called Vanessa and asked her to ride with me over to his house. We arrived on Love Joy Road around eight-thirty Friday night. Derron came to the door and when he opened the door he said, "Welcome." We went in and I was excited and nervous at the same time, because I wanted so much for this guy to be long term. We entered the living room and sat down. Derron offered us drinks and of course, my cousin took one and I sat quietly on the sofa smiling yet screaming on the inside because I felt so free from married life. Derron came and stood over me and held out his hand to lead me somewhere. I was more than willing to follow so I stood up and put my hand in his's and needless to say he led me to his bedroom and closed the door behind us. I sat on the bed and then he guided his 3x t-shirt off his tall, long upper body. I watched in silence, biting my bottom lip and undressing him with my eyes from his waist down. He finally took off his pants and stood in front of me looking like a tall glass of chocolate milk that I could only drink half of, because I'm so petite in size.

I noticed that Derron shaved his pubic hair and I asked him about it. He then told me that he shaved them to make his dick look bigger. I asked him not to do it anymore because it looked kind of gay to me. He agreed and then asked me to undress and lay back on the bed... I did. He then asked me to take my pussy lips and spread them apart... I did. He got on the bed and sat up on his knees and he spread my legs apart as if he was going to break a wish bone, and he then put his long silvery tongue dead in the center of my tootsie roll pop and ate my pussy like I had never ever encountered. I shivered, quivered, and had a lions, tigers and bears climax! He dick became so hard the he couldn't lie down on the bed became it was sticking straight out. By that time, I was having coochie earthquakes and couldn't move until he tried to ease his colossal dick inside of me. I somehow created a new way to run. I slided up the bed backward. He caught me by my leg and pulled me back down and erotically guided his big chocolate dick into my pussy. I screamed at first because it felt like something was trying to break through a tiny entrance, but then he looked at me and started sucking on my bottom lip. I assumed it was to distract me from the pain that I was experiencing. Shortly after it was in, it felt as if he had filled up all the room with his dick that a a sign needed to hang on my clitoris reading, "No Vacancies." He filled me up to the point that I felt that I had to pee. His dick was so big that he could have sky lifted my ass to the toilet without having to take it out. I was locked down on it, and it was so tight that I felt confident that I wasn't going to fall off. Derron kept saying to me, "Baby look at you; look at you. Do you see you? Oooh … Seneca, you're taking all daddi's dick." By the time he had finished fucking me I was dickmatized, traumatized, and my eyes were wide shut because he had fucked me for a good three days … damn I meant hours. He was training me to take it all and at the same time being very gentle. You know after the pain comes pleasure or maybe it's the other way around. When it was over, I didn't know my name, how I had got there, or the year I was born. Yes, it was that intense!

After calming down, I remembered that my cousin was sitting in the living room and since it was my first time experiencing such a big dick, I wanted my cousin to see it. It's not that I wanted to share it, I just wanted my cousin to have something else to gossip talk about it. Since, she was one of those chicks that couldn't hold water in her mouth without spilling it. If you had something to tell, you better not have told Vanessa because everybody and their mama would know about it in two point five seconds. I asked Derron to walk to the kitchen to get me a soda, but he had to pass the living room where she was sitting just so she could see it. Derron was slipping his pants on and I stopped him and told him keep them off. He didn't ask any questions but just proceeded to do what was requested of him. I didn't care about my cousin seeing him because I knew she wasn't the type to desire anything I had and I trust her. Besides, I didn't love Derron; we were just having fun. He walked out in front of her, but my cousin was somewhat shy and Derron said she didn't even look. When he put the soda on the nightstand I began sucking his dick until he came all over my face, neck and chest. I believe he was surprised to see a little woman taking his dick. In fact… I surprised my damn self.

CHAPTER 5
INTERDICTION

My life had changed right before my eyes. I was caught between the old and familiar and something new and unfamiliar. I was living a double life with two men who were very similar in some ways but so different in character. I felt trapped and just really wanted to come out and let Tony know that I had met someone, but then … how could I? He was still my legal husband that I had three kids with, yet I was dying to tell him because of the type of woman I am. It was hard to lie about my feelings when I knew that I was falling for someone and I'm usually I am in it all the way or not at all. In this situation, I was in it all the way. I was feeling myself gravitate towards Derron a lot and I have always been terrible at hiding in my feelings inside. That's why it was so hard not to come out and let Tony know that he was in fact losing me. Besides, I didn't want to send him over the top with that kind of news and I didn't know for sure that I was the only one rocking Derron's bed. My life became so crazy and Derron was demanding more time, more sex, more answers, and pressing me to leave my husband. The questions kept coming like, "when could you spend the night? When can I meet my kids? When can you come over to cook my dinner? He made sure that although I was still married to Tony, he was going to number one or nothing at all in my life. I started leaving work around 4:45 pm every day, even though I was scheduled to get off at 5:00 pm just so I had enough time to make it over to Derron's house to cook, clean and sex him down; then I would go home to take care of the kids and repeat most of the same chores that I'd done at my baby's house – except for the sex. I began to see to different between my man and my husband. I would observe my new man smoking weed and he didn't act anything like my husband. My husband would go crazy if he didn't get some weed … or some other shit. I didn't care about anything Tony was doing or saying because Derron would have taken care of me way before I got home and I made sure that my man was pleased and well satisfied in return. Nothing Tony could have done or said was going to impinge on me. I found myself really distancing myself from Tony and anything that concerned him.

Three weeks had passed and Derron and I were getting more and more acquainted. There wasn't a day that passed when I didn't think about him. I would be riding in the car with my husband and this song by Lauren Hill called, *You're Too Good Too Be True* would by playing on a CD and I would just look out of the car window and smile. Even when Tony was raising the worst hell, it didn't bother me because my mind was engaged in all the encounters I have had with Derron. Sometimes I would just giggle to myself about something Derron had done or said to make me laugh and it would leave Tony wondering what was so damn funny. Every week I found myself making my way over to Love Joy Road, staying the whole day and going to church with Derron, out to dinner and back to his house to make love to him in ways I thought could be illegal. His dick was the biggest I've ever encountered, so it wasn't long before I was hooked, lined and conquered. At times I would have to count back one-one thousand, two-two thousand, three-three thousand just to keep from being wooed.

Derron kept pressuring me to spend the night at his house and although I wanted to it seemed nearly impossible because Tony's high never lasted long enough for me to make that move. I swore to Derron that I would work on staying over one night, but I couldn't make any promises. I wanted nothing more than to please him because he was what I felt a strong man should be; a take-charge type that wanted things done speedily before he finished smoking his Newport cigarette. But that's another thing that drew me to him. He had my respect. He made decisions and stuck to them; he was everything that I lacked and his weaknesses were my strengths. He had confidence, charisma, a sense of humor and wasn't afraid to tell me no, but would dick me down for good behavior.

On the other hand, Tony was too simple. I was able to run over him like I was on the I-285 North, pulled over in the emergency lane, change my tire and keep it rolling. He didn't have much of a backbone because he was the type of man that used his fists to keep him in the game. I respected a man who was strong mentally and not just physically. I didn't particularly like it when a man uses his physical strength to beat up a woman because of his own insecurities. Derron's only method of hitting was to hit my pussy from the back in his doggy style position. He was what I called a gentle giant thug. He showed me love in public and would always call me his baby, but he was daddy at night, which I spelled **D.A.D.D.I.** Also, Derron and Tony were totally opposite when it came to appearances. Derron was tall and skinny with no facial hair, long braids and a pointed nose. Tony, on the other hand wasn't as tall, had facial hair, short wavy hair, and was muscle bound built. It was a big difference and when Derron and I were in public, we stood out.

So it was the small things that I appreciated, more than the materialistic things that I had in the past with Tony before his drug habit completely took over.

My big break finally came when I was able to sway Tony into trading my temporary freedom from him and the kids for enough money for his weed. I felt so nervous and energized about what was going to happen once I stayed the night with Derron. It kind of takes me back to a scene I once saw in the movie *The Color Purple,* when Sophia had just been released from prison during the Christmas holidays and she hadn't seen her children in eight years. Her white slave owner told her, "Sophia, I'm taking you home tomorrow for Christmas to see your kids and you can stay all day... Yes, all day!"

Yes, it was that tremendous and that was the only metaphor I could think of to explain how much that one night of freedom meant to me. It was agreed upon and my sexual adventure began. Derron and I became closer and closer and my feelings grew swiftly as the two of us worked our way into a whirlwind of sex, partying, fine dining and traveling.

One evening Derron called me on my cellphone to announce that he was having a Christmas party, and that he wanted me to come. I was quite keyed up about it because I would get a chance to see his friends and observe his personality and behavior around his people.

On December 19, Derron hosted his first Christmas party at his house and I took along with me a female friend named, Chiquitta. I wore a black swing dress that was like something you would see Pebble wearing on *The Flinstones*. Upon our arrival at Derron's apartment I touched up my makeup, and then we got out of the car and walked up to the door and rang the doorbell. When Derron opened the door his eyes lit up as if he had radar vision that saw straight through my dress. I set my eyes on his tall, slender, toned body and gladly entered, with Chiquita following. "Hi baby, this is Chiquita," I said introducing her as he grabbed my hand. Chiquita look up and nodded her head to say hi and Derron threw up a Westside hand signal to her in return for speaking to him. She and I both looked at each other with confusion and kept walking. Passing the kitchen entrance on the right and the living room straight ahead, I could see that there were several guests, but I knew none of them. Derron led us into the living room holding my hand and then he announced to everyone my position by saying, "Hey everybody, this lil' mama here is my new baby ... and oh, this is her friend, Quitta Right?" He turned towards Chiquitta to confirm her name and then laughed out loud because he had almost forgotten it. Everyone laughed because Chiquitta gave him a funny, frowning look and then one by one each of them came to greet me and introduce them selves.

I sat down and Derron offered me a drink. "Oh no, thank you baby, I don't drink, remember?" Derron quickly apologized and said, "That's some good shit. My bad, baby." I told him that my friend might want a drink, though. He went and got her a Corona and then he returned to the kitchen three more times to get her some Hennessey and coke, and finally a Long Island iced tea. She became intoxicated very quickly, so I asked him not to give her anything else. He respected my request and closed down the bar on her ass. As a matter of a fact, she so many drinks that she end up falling to sleep on his sofa. Although Chiquita was kind of embarrassing to me, everyone understood and just overlooked her.

Derron continued to host the party with such magnetism and he managed to keep his eyes on me at all times. I gave Derron a crystal, heart shaped, swan ornament to go on his Christmas tree. The swans were kissing inside of the heart and to my surprise it was actually the only ornament on the whole tree.

I needed to go the restroom so I informed Derron, because his bedroom door was closed and I had to go through there in order to get to the restroom. While I was sitting on the toilet, Derron came into the restroom and stood over me. I told Derron that he needed to go back out there with his guests. He replied by saying that they were okay. As I was about to get up and wipe myself, he began to unzip his jeans and then he pulled his dick out and put in my mouth. It was so intensified because there were so many people in the house; the music was loud and I could hear everyone laughing and talking. Sucking his dick gave me pleasure because it was so big and not only that, I enjoyed the foreplay of sneaking around with him. After about a minute or so, Derron loaded his dick back into his pants and went out to entertain his guest. I just sat there for a while with my wet pussy dripping. I could hear the drips then it was quiet for second, and then it would drip again in the toilet as I tried to get myself back together. When I came out of the restroom, the party was ending and everyone was leaving except for my friend who had come along with me. It was around three in the morning, so I assisted the ladies there with the cleanup. Chiquita was sleeping on the sofa and I woke her up and told her that we would be leaving shortly, but she could barely make out what I was saying and fell back asleep.   "All right, ladies I'll finish up the rest tomorrow, but thank y'all for the help, folks," Derron said to the ladies in the kitchen as he stretched and yawned. They turned the water off, put the broom down and flicked the kitchen light out. "I'll see you tomorrow Derron and it was nice meeting you, Seneca," they yelled as they walked out of the front door. Derron saw them to the door and locked it. He then gestured for me to come into the bedroom, where he fucked me until the sun began to come up. All anyone could hear was, "Get it Daddi, Fuck me Daddi, Look at you, Daddi!" coming from my mouth. All the moaning and groaning must have finally woken up Chiquita. She knocked on the door and began calling my name. "Seneca, Seneca, I' m ready to go." Derron yelled out, "She'll be coming in a minute." I giggled because I didn't know whether he meant that I was coming or cumming. Chiquita continued to knock on the door repeating the same thing over and over and Derron kept stroking and humping me and yelling out to her, "She's coming!"

After an hour had passed, I came out of the room and Chiquita was asleep on the couch again. I woke her up and said, "Are you ready?" She got up and didn't answer me. I assumed that she was pissed off because she was ready to go or because it wasn't her in the bedroom with my man. Nevertheless, I kissed Derron goodbye and we left.

Throughout the whole drive home and even when dropping Chiquita off at home, she never spoke to me again. It was obvious that she was upset with me, but I hadn't given her a specific time that I would be leaving and she seemed to been having a great time sleeping, so I took the chance to spend time with the man I wanted to be with. She wasn't in the dark about anything but she acted like I had cut her a raw deal or something. I probably would have been upset too, but not to the point that I would have cut my friend off. My friendship with her was over, but my sex life with my new man lived on.

CHAPTER 6
BEING PRESSURED TO LEAVE

It was the end of December and Derron had officially introduced me to everyone as his new girl. Frankly, I was okay with that because I was feeling him on that level. One evening we decided to go back to the club we originally met. We met at his house and I got in the car with him and we headed to the club. My cellphone started ringing off the hook. I took out my phone to see who was calling at one in the morning and it was Tony. I told Derron who was calling and asked him to turn the music down for a second. After he did, I answered the phone in a low voice. "Sen, where are you?" Tony said. "I'm on my way to the club Tony. Why what's up?" I answered. "Man ... I believe you're with a nigga. You need to bring you ass home!" Tony screamed. I looked over at Derron while he was driving and he seemed to remain cool as ice. I answered, "No, I'll be there later!"

This was strange because Tony had never called me like this when I was out and it scared the fuck out of me. I started thinking maybe he had caught on to what's going on and perhaps he's going to try to fight with me when I get home. So I started talking very softly to him on the phone. Tony kept insisting that I come home and made me do crazy shit like roll the window down, roll the window up, open and close the car doors, just to see if I was with someone during the time we were on the phone. He also made threats to kill my dog, Roger, if I didn't come home. Although I knew he wouldn't do that, Derron thought it was serious enough for me to leave him as soon as possible. Just so I wouldn't have to face some extreme fighting. Derron became very pissed off with me. I could tell by the look on his face that he was not appreciating this game that I was playing with Tony. When I got off the phone, Derron said, "Look. It's like this, if you're my woman, then you will not be answering to no other nigga, but me! I know that's your husband, but you are my woman and he will not have you acting like a damn puppet!" I sat there in shock and wanted nothing more than to submit to him. He called me his woman, I said silently to myself and then I smirked. He turned the music up and we continued making our way to Club Mirage.

At the club, we sat down at the bar for Derron to order his Corona and then we moved over to a table. I got up to go to the ladies room and Derron remained at the table drinking and listening to the music. I must have stayed in the ladies room for about twenty minutes or so talking to the other ladies and touching up my diamond lipgloss. When suddenly, there was a knock on the ladies room door and a deep voice yelled "Seneca." It was Derron. I answered, "Here I come baby," but just as I was turning to grab the door handle to walk out. Derron busted in the door and said, "Why the hell did you leave me out there that long?"

"I … I was coming baby," I said in a bewildered voice. The ladies in the restroom were looking puzzled. One lady was actually in the middle of pulling up her pantyhose up when he busted in and she still had her pantyhose thigh-high when I looked over at her. "Let's go, right now!" I walked swiftly out of the restroom with humiliation written all on my face. I felt Derron had got upset about the phone incident that happened early in the car, so I brushed it off.

When we got to the car, Derron said, "Don't you ever leave me like that again! If I wanted to come alone to a club I would have done so … you digg?" "Baby, baby … I'm sorry. I didn't realize how long I took. I was only gone for twenty minutes," I replied.

"Just don't let it happen again, alright?" he said as he rubbed his hand across my face. Derron lit up a blunt but it didn't bother me because he seemed to be so cool and in control of himself while smoking. He was controlling it and it was not in control of him.

Afterwards, we drove to his house and made love until about five in the morning. He fell asleep and I got up to get dressed and then I woke him up and told him that I was leaving. He told me to be careful and to call him once I made it home. Once I arrived, Tony was on the back porch smoking. I got undressed and I went to sleep.

CHAPTER 7
NO LOOKING BACK

Christmas had passed and Derron and I exchanged gifts about a week later because I was spending Christmas at home with my kids and he went back home to visit in family. I bought him some cologne and he bought me a much-needed cellphone, because the one I had belonged to Tony and he would take away it whenever he felt like it. These were the first presents we gave to each other and it meant a lot to me. We decided to bring in the New Year together, so I knew I had to get a plan together to get out of the house. Tony was so into smoking weed and had just added eating cocaine to his menu, so by this time it was a lot easier to get out because he was always fucked up and not paying attention to me.

I made arrangements for my kids to stay with my mother for the evening and I got dressed and made my way over to Love Joy Street. Derron wore this brown and golden suit. He was so damn fine and I wore a long cocktail dress. We set out for the Vegas Night Club with one of his friends and his girl. We arrived at the club around 9:00 pm and every woman was there will their man. I was so excited to be there with him, and my adrenaline had passed orbit. At the club Derron had a Long Island Iced Tea, Corona, and Hennessey and Coke, while I sipped on my coca-cola with one cherry in it. We walked around the club enjoying each other and the company of his friends. The time was getting closer to bring in the New Year and I was happier than I ever had been before. I excused myself to go to the restroom and Derron told me to hurry back because it was about fifteen minutes till the stroke of the New Year. I ran up three flights of stairs to use to the restroom and just about when I was flushing the toilet I heard everyone counting down on the intercom ten, nine, eight, seven, six ... I quickly washed my hands and ran out of the restroom and back down the stairs, but as I was coming down Derron was running up the stairs towards me. We met each other on the middle set of stairs on the count of one, and then we kissed as everyone screamed, "Happy New Year!"

It was magical and I believed that that night I fell in love with him, and for some reason I knew Derron felt it too. We walked through the club hand in hand, which was unusual because you did not see many couples holding hands.

His friend walked up to us and started talking about Derron's kids. When we met Derron had mentioned that he had two sons in Kentucky and that was it. His friend, Darius asked him, when was the last time you've seen your daughter. I looked at him and said, "Daughter?" Derron said, "I'll explain later." Later that morning, we sat down and he explained that he hadn't mentioned his daughter because he felt that she was not his. I just went along with whatever he told me and left it at that.

We begin going to the church that he had been a member of for three years almost every Sunday. I really liked the church. However, there was something very different about his church. The pastor preached very well but he gave me the feeling that he could probably be gay. One day during the 11:30 service while the pastor was preaching, I nudged Derron and whispered to him, "The pastor is preaching like he's gay." Derron didn't say anything, and we continued listening to the sermon. I started noticing that just about all his sermons had something in them about defending homosexuals.

After we left church, Derron said that he had heard some rumors, but he didn't know if it was true or not. Although I thought it was strange to see my long time gay friend, David and his lover at the church. I didn't make mention of it because Derron made it a point at the beginning of our relationship that he wanted a woman that attended church and didn't want to be around negative people. I didn't want to come across as negative, so I put my wonderng thoughts in the back of my head and focused on why I was there. Besides it was an honor for me to be there because I always wanted to go to church, but my marriage with Tony was in so much chaos that I was distracted and discouraged from attending.

Derron began pressuring me to be with him all the time and I was really feeling a need to just say fuck it and leave my marriage. After all, there was nothing holding me there. Tony's drug habit had grown totally out of control, and I really didn't take any blame for that became I didn't put it to his mouth. I just provided him with the money in order to get what he wanted, so I could get what I wanted. I mean, we had kids and had been together for years, but the relationship was pretty much.

Nevertheless, I told Derron that I couldn't leave so soon because I had to prepare and besides that I was scared. I really didn't know what was out there, and not knowing if I could care for my three kids by myself kept me enmeshed in my dysfunctional marriage. I always knew how to love, but I had never learned the art of letting go. I promised Derron that I would leave and I needed him to be patient with me and give me more time. At first he was okay with that, but he grew tired of waiting, which made it harder for him to deal with the fact that I was still living in the same house with my husband. Although we had stopped sleeping in the same bedroom and didn't have sex anymore, Derron still felt like it was too much for him to handle. As twisted as it may sound, I would have felt guilty for having sex with my husband because in my eyes it would have been like I was cheating on my boyfriend. Derron continued to complain about me staying with Tony, and since I didn't leave when he felt I should have, he end up leaving me.

The break-up bothered me at first, but my life went back to being normally abnormal. I went to work, took care of the kids, fussed, cussed and watched Tony's fiend scheming continue. Although I was in love with Derron I was able to let him go because I was in fact caught between living two live. As much as I didn't want to let him go I knew I had to, because he wouldn't have stayed with me while I was still there with Tony. Also, his friends, mainly one of his so-called females, tried to persuade him to leave me because she felt I wasn't going to leave my marriage. She was one of the girls I met at the Christmas party. Even then, she seemed to be under him a little too much to be just a friend, but I try to pay it no mind until now. I believed it was more so because she had had an affair with him a while back and that she herself was married. The differences that she and I had was that she was married to a good guy named, John who did not do drugs or beat on her. I had met him briefly at the Christmas party and as I can recall he looked quite uncomfortable at the Christmas party as well. He was a hard worker and wanted nothing more than to be with his family. It was settled. Derron's friends had convinced him to leave me along and he went back to living his life.

CHAPTER 8
MEANT TO BE

It was about two o'clock am on a cold January morning and although Derron and I had stopped seeing each other, I was still sleeping in a separate room from Tony. The cellphone that Derron had bought me was on the battery charger in the kitchen. It was ringing, and since Tony was up getting high he decided to answer it. I didn't expect it to be Derron because he had stopped calling me and besides he knew not to call especially that time of morning.

When Tony answered the phone and a man's voice on the other end said, "I'm sorry for calling your home this early in the morning, but you see your wife Seneca is a friend of mine and I'm in jail. I know that she works for the police department and I wanted to see if she could help me out." Tony did take to kindly to this. After all it was another man on the phone asking for me. Tony immediately went on a rampage of yelling and cussing him out. His loud voice woke up me and the kids. When I heard the conversation from afar I immediately knew it was Derron on the phone and I said to myself what in hell is he doing? So I pretended like I was asleep because I knew Tony was going to make his way back to my room to bawl me out about this sudden phone call.

Suddenly, Tony stormed into my room and flicked on the light. I tightly shut my eyes and I heard him yell out, "Sene... Seneca!" I said, "What?" very softly as if he had just awakened me out of a deep sleep. He cried, "This guy is on the phone saying he took you from me." I jumped up and said, "Man, stop damn playing. Ain't nobody one on the phone!" He continued to yell and I continued to deny until I thought of away to get out of this shit. Finally, I told him to give me the phone. When I got the phone my heart was racing speedily inside of my gown and my brain had to wake up and get me out of this shit. I was holding the phone very firmly just in case I had to use it as a weapon then I said, "Who is this?" A deep voice answered you know who this is. I recognized Derron's voice. Yelling through the phone I shouted, "David! David! Why are you playing with Tony on the phone?" lauging out loud. David was a gay friend of mine from way, way back. Tony knew of him, but had never met him. I said to Tony, "Here's the phone, I'm going back to bed." He left out of the room with the phone still up to his ear. I just could only imagine what Derron was telling him on the phone, but I knew I had to play it off to keep my ass out of a fight, and with Tony's abusive background I was scared that he might just kill the me and my kids. Tony came back into mt room with the same accusations and I continued to deny, deny, deny. Tony wasn't backing down, so I got up out of bed and walked through the house pretending to act upset with him for accusing me in order to make my side look real. Tony continued to get louder and the kids were getting scared so I called the police to come to the house. When they arrived Tony went into his victim's state of mind and the police actually took his side, believe it or not. Now it was about 5:00 am, and I hadn't been back to sleep so I decided to lie down after the police left. Tony had somewhat calmed down and Derron was still calling, but every time he called I pressed the ignore button on the phone because I didn't want Tony to start up again.

About fifteen minutes had passed since the police had left, when they suddenly came back and this time bust through the front door and arrested Tony for an outstanding warrant for a bad check. I guess it had been called in shortly after they left. "This shit is crazy!" I said, running towards my kids' bedroom to check on them. When I looked in the room my baby girl was crying, so I told my oldest girl to put the pacifier in her mouth and to stay put and told hem that I would be right back. "What in the hell is going on here?" I yelled out. Now, my husband and my boyfriend were locked up at the same time. I called Derron back on his cellphone. Ironically, they had allowed him to keep his cellphone with him in the jail cell. It's like he could charm anyone to get whatever he wanted. When he answered the phone I said,"Derron, why did you do that, you could have gotten me and my girls killed!?"

"I did not start anything with him he came off on me," he yelled back at me.

"Anyway, why are you in jail?" I asked. The phone grew silent.

Screaming out his name I cried, "Derron Derron." All I could hear was the echo of the cell that he was in and then he grasped and said, "Uh, uh… D.U.I. But-but it's ain't true. I'm not dru…I'm not fucking drunk! I only had two beers," he yelled in a slurred voice. I went on the ask him where was he coming from and he said, "Club Mirage." He also added that he was upset about us and couldn't sleep so he went to the club.

With admiration I said, "Damn Daddi that's sweet, yet crazy. You know I was thinking about us to. By the way, the police just locked Tony up."

"Good! You better not go get the nigga' out of jail!" he said.

Hesitating, I responded, "Look, I have three kids! Are you going to step up to the plate?"

He answered, "Yes," in a confident, but indecisive, voice. I then held the phone for a minute and I said, "Okay then, fine. I won't go get his ass out".

Derron then mentioned in a sarcastic tone, "Oh yeah, thanks for calling me your gay friend, David." I giggled and told him that he put me in a tight spot, so I had to make up something. This is when I knew I was truly in love with Derron because in the past Tony had been locked up several times and every single time I was there to bail him out.

The sun was coming up and I began getting ready for work. After dropping the kids off at school, I called to check on Derron and to make sure he had gotten out of jail. I went to work and got on the Internet to search for another house for my kids and I to move into while Tony was still locked up. I found a house about twenty-five miles away from the house we were living in. The following day I went to view the house and sign the leasing papers. Once everything was settled, I prepared to move as fast I could and I transferred my kids to the new county school system. I had finally grown the balls to leave my marriage because I had someone behind me to give me the push and courage I needed to get over this fence. In all truth, I'd wanted to leave him, but didn't know how and I didn't have the confidence to because Tony had over the years instilled a mindset in me that no one would ever want me because I had kids. However, looking beyond my doubt in a strange but tentative way; I felt that God had orchestrated the set up early that morning to help me to get out of that abusive relationship. I have always heard the saying that, "What the devil meant for evil; God would make it for your good," That's the quote that came to my mind when this whole situation went down. Perhaps Tony was going to end up killing me or I would end up killing him... I don't know. Don't get me wrong, I'm not saying that God closed his eyes to adultery and fornication, but he knew my situation and chose Derron as a guide to help me to get out of something that wasn't good for me.

On the day Derron was released from jail, he was getting ready to leave for Mardi Gras in New Orleans. I didn't know anything about the trip until later on that evening. He said that it was a trip that he and his friends had already planned; they had reservations. I was scared because he was leaving and Tony was gone, and I was alone handling everything by myself, which was new to me. It was the first time I had lived on my own with my kids. I felt alone at times, but mentally and physically free, and I talked to Derron almost every day while he was away. I was now living my life as a single mom and Derron's girl.

A week had passed and I had not heard a word from Tony. Derron was on his way home to Atlanta, and I was eager to see him. He called to let me know he was coming over to see the house. My kids all accepted him because I had spoken very highly of him. This was actually the first time he ever met my girls.

We went out to dinner and once we got back to the house we made love. The next morning I went to work and Derron slept in late until about noon. When I arrived at work, I had several messages from Tony; he had begun sending me emails from a secret location. I knew something was up and someone had to have shown him how to use a computer, because he wasn't computer-literate. Later on, I found out that after he got out of jail, he went back to the house to find that it was empty. That's when he lost it and checked himself into a mental hospital. I felt bad at first, but I was happy that I was out for good and I had no intention of going back to him.   Thereafter, my relationship with Derron was in full swing. We spent every waking moment together and our nights were filled with going to dinner, movies, birthday parties, clubs and everything else under the sun. Life seemed to have been going so well between us and at that time I vowed to myself that I would never argue with another man again. "When Derron is fire, I will be water," I kept telling myself. I submitted to his commands and felt good about doing it because I was allowed to be the poodle that I was all along. I had someone who could just handle things and step up to the plate for once. It was nice to have a real man running the show, and I was able to sit back and let my man be the man. Sometimes we would have minor problems, but nothing that had me in fear of the relationship.

CHAPTER 9
MOVING TO FAST

Derron did begin wandering off from time to time to the clubs with his friends and not answering his phone at night. One night while Derron was out I called Belinda on the phone and mentioned to her what was going on between Derron and I. She then said, "Well, Seneca, I did not want to get in your business and you know I'm no hater, right?"

"Right… Right," I said slowly, sweat forming on my forehead because I did not know what was going to come from her mouth next.

"You're my girl… so I'm just trying to look out for you." She continued.

"What is it, girl!" I said in an anxious and scared voice. She went on to say that she knew a female name Candy that Derron used to fuck with and that this girl had told her that I wouldn't last long because Derron was into hoodrat chicks. These were the kind of girls that fight and fuck at the drop of a dime. Who had a gold teeth; talk straight ghetto and smoke weed.

Well surely that did not describe me, so I felt that she could have been lying about him because I was just the opposite of what she was describing. Although, I sometimes became skeptical about him being honest with me regarding his outings, because I knew that once I doubted his love for me it would cause problems. So I kept my thoughts to myself and besides whatever he was doing in the streets wasn't going to hold his attention too long. Let's put it another way, I took care of him at home and I wasn't about to leave him for nothing or no one. One night when he had gone out to the club and I had a dream about him that was so vivid and real. I dreamt that I was in my new house and it was very, very dark. The hallway was long and there was a closet on the left side that wasn't there in real life. In the dream I heard gun shots and I hurried up to my oldest daughter's room to check on her. When I looked into her room; she was sitting on the floor with two little toddler boys. I said to her, "I didn't tell you that you could baby sit. Take those kids home." I closed the door and began walking back down the hall to my bedroom. At that time, I looked to the left and there was Derron in the closet with a very bright light hanging over his head. Derron was trying on my husband's clothing and he had on blue sweater that was much too small for him. When he saw me he said with an evil, mean look on his face, "You need to clean out this closet" In the dream, I smiled at him and didn't respond but just continued walking to my bedroom that was located at the end of the dark hall. When I went to lie down on the bed, a big tongue came out from under my bed and began licking me all over very sexually. The strange thing is that I liked it, but then it started pulling me underneath the bed. I begin praying to God and repeating the Lord's Prayer over and over. The evil, enticing tongue released my legs and arms and I woke up out of the dream in a soggy sweat with a racing heartbeat. That dream was so real that it scared the hell out of me. I woke my kids up in the middle of the night and pulled them into bed with me; I was too afraid to look under my bed that whole night. I blew the dream off for a bit, but deep down inside of me I felt that perhaps this dream had a meaning. I mean, I loved the way Derron did me but the correlation to the clothes and kids was far beyond my understanding. What did the dream mean? I didn't know, but I was just glad that it was over.

CHAPTER 10
THE OTHER GEMINI SHOWED UP

My March birthday had just passed when Derron took me to a beautiful restaurant called the Sundial, inside the Western Peachtree Hotel. We had such a lovely time that evening. All the white girls in the hotel thought that he was a famous basketball player and I was a model. In fact, Derron had allowed me to get back into modeling because I expressed to him that it was my passion. Every time we went out, we stood out amongst every couple that was in the club, mall, movie or restaurant. I guess it was because I was so short and petite and he was so tall and skinny. After leaving the restaurant, we drove to Buckhead to Vision's nightclub to party.

Two weeks after my birthday Derron hung out late for five days straight with his friends. It did not dawn on me that his birthday was right around the corner. Things were becoming a little shaky between him and I and Derron wanted to be alone more for some reason. I had always been so submissive to him and didn't give him any problems, so I was confused about what was happening to us, but I gave him his space. Although I felt something wasn't right, I kept right on being submissive to him and taking care of his needs whenever he called on me. Derron begin drinking more, yelling at me more about any and everything and smoking weed regularly every day. If this weed appetite was a part of him at the beginning of the relationship, I never knew it and he did not show it. He even started going to point of putting me on restrictions. He had the *"Don't Call Me Today Restriction"*; the *"Go Home Restriction"* and the most unforgettable restriction was the one he called the *"Dick Punishment Restriction."* He knew he had me sprung so he would use these so-called restrictions as means to punish me for whatever he felt I had done wrong. I tried to be all I could be for him, but it seemed like everything I did was now getting on his nerves. I started questioning myself and walking on eggshells just so I wouldn't upset him in any kind of way. Around the end of May, Derron decided to break up with me for absolutely no reason at all. I backed off because I wanted to give him time and room to think about this drastic decision that he was making, hoping that my absence from him would encourage him to change his mind. It almost drove me crazy not to see him. I tried talking to him from time to time and continued to be patient, but nothing seemed to be working.

Interesting enough, his birthday was the week after he broke up with me. I had already bought him a birthday present before the break up and very much wanted him to have it, so I called him and asked if I could drop his present off. He said it would be cool. When I arrived the door was unlocked like he would usually leave it when he knew I was coming over. I walked into the living room where he was sitting in the dark watching basketball. "Hi" he said in a very low tone. With a glow on my face, I walked over to him very quietly and bent down to kiss him. Instead of taking a seat next to him on the sofa, I knelt down between his legs and laid my head of his washboard shirtless abs. He rubbed the back of my hair with one hand and then he helped me up on the sofa to sit next to him. Holding back tears, I said, happy birthday in a cracking voice and gave him his present. "Thank you, he said, with a half-smirk on his face. While he began opening the small box wrapped in red paper, I sighed with what I call emotional anxiety and held my head down. After taking the wrapping off and he did not open the box. He pushed my chin up with his finger and said in an overwhelmed voice, "Baby, Baby ... you didn't have to do this." I stared at him with tears in my eyes and replied, "No, no baby. I... I wanted to." I went on to say that I understood that we were no longer a couple, but I loved him so deeply and I wanted to give it to him. Actually, I didn't understand, but I was so happy to see him that I didn't even think about stating my case with him or arguing because I just wanted to enjoy that moment. He opened the gift box and discovered a beautiful white gold men bracelet. "Damn baby! How much you spend on this?" he asked. "Oh, It's not important but you are and that's why I got it for you," I replied. After he opened the present, I hurried off the sofa and told him that I was leaving now because I had to take care of some things. But the reason I left is because I did not want him to feel guilty or obligated to me because I bought him a birthday present. He walked me to door and then I looked up at him and he bent down to kiss me. Later on that evening, Derron called me and began thanking me again for the bracelet. He said he had shown it to everyone and they thought it was beautiful. He mentioned that his friends had told him that I must have really loved him to buy him something that expensive and they couldn't believe he let me go. He went on to say that I was the only one that got him something for his birthday and that he would call me later. Strangely enough, Derron called me back later that evening and said that he had been thinking about us and that our relationship was back on.

"Back on?" I said to myself. Back on, back off ... Damn! What is with his "Type A personality" I thought to myself. His Dr. Jeckle and Mr. Hyde act was driving me crazy and often left me mystified. The two months on, one month off relationship was getting old and more than that it was becoming mentally sick for me! Although I complained to myself and to my friends, I wasn't about to stand up to him. He had molded me already and I knew how far to go with him. Besides, I had made up my mind that I was going to stick this out no matter what. So just to make sure I didn't do whatever I'd done to cause Derron to break up with me I started analyzing everything I could have possibly done that would upset him. "Did I talk too much?" "Did I not talk enough?" "I did sex him right the last couple times" "I'm not hood-rattish or ghetto enough."

All kinds of questions and answers started running through my mind. I just wanted to figure this shit out and make sure I didn't do or start doing what I was or wasn't supposed to.

Two months later, our relationship seemed to be on target and everything was going well. Derron was spending more time with me and the girls. We all went on a family vacation together to Myrtle Beach, with his kids included. Derron started investing in me, or should I say in the relationship. I believed he saw me as wife material and he decided that he was going to give it one hundred percent. Later on that year, he bought me a nearly brand new truck that I really didn't want, but for whatever reason he insisted. He was getting ready to get a new Cadillac and said he didn't want his baby riding around in a hooty car while he had a new car. I appreciated the offer but I really didn't want to accept it, at least not yet. It seemed like a bit much for quite a new relationship and I did not know what was behind it all. He was very persistent, and even when I kept telling him that I could wait until next year he continued to offer.

It was the end of September income tax season was only a few months away. I was looking forward to filing my taxes to purchase my own car, but the two new vehicles were soon to be in our possession. The day we went to sign the papers for the vehicles, Derron told the dealership salesman that he was about to propose to me. Well, he did just that and the salesman announced the proposal over the intercom at the dealership. Derron had made me so happy and he seemed to love me so much. Some of his friends, but mainly his friend Kenar told him that it wasn't a good idea to get me the car. Derron was cool with the situation, but I was still uneasy about it.

Our friends seemed somewhat jealous and envious because we were doing so well together, and more than that, we were happy. Then all of sudden, again, Derron started hanging more with his friends in his new Caddy. His attitude became a little more arrogant, and he became extremely controlling. He stopped wanting to be with me as much, and when his friends were around I wasn't allowed to come over. Sometimes I would spend the weekend with him and his phone at home would not ring at all. When I left on Sundays after church to go home, his female friends would come over later. I knew this because I would call and he would tell me that he was smoking a blunt with Shania. I didn't like it, but I couldn't do anything about it because he would put me in check, or sometimes put me on restrictions for talking back.

Other times, he would hang out with his boys and when I called him that evening or the next day, he wouldn't answer his cellphone or his home phone. I knew something was wrong because it started happening on a regular basis. As time went on Derron grew colder and colder with no remorse for the distance and the mean, harsh things he said to keep me in line or keep me away. Since I was in love with him and didn't want to lose him, I obeyed and rarely talked back. When I was with Tony I had to fight all the time with him, and for him. It was a part of me that I didn't like because it took me out of my character. I had to nearly walk a tightrope, or on eggshells, because he had become so damn hard on me. He started complaining about my clothes, my friends, and my parenting skills and I had to ask for permission to participate in any modeling or movie events. He didn't like the fact that I was in the modeling industry and he was very insecure about me being around celebrity guys.

Derron would lie compulsively and thought he was pulling the wool over my eyes about his whereabouts and phone calls. Sometimes I would play the dumb fox role, playing ignorant to a situation in order to gain more insight or information about it. I only played a fool to catch his dumb ass. All along I knew what he was doing, who he was doing it with and how he was doing it. I suspected him of cheating so I would play the number game on his phone. When he turned his phone off for hours, I would call his phone and it would go straight to his voicemail box. I then picked his voicemail password and checked his messages. I became so good at it that I even taught my girls, Belinda and Vanessa how to do it. Although I knew what he was doing I didn't say anything, because I did want to let him go and wanted to show him that I would be submissive to him, unlike all the hoodrats he was dealing with. But I was actually being someone that I wasn't. Back in the day, I would handle shit like this head on, choke the shit out of someone and ask questions later. I didn't want to re-live that type of behavior, so I decided to think rationally and made a choice to deal with it differently. Tony had made me insecure in our relationship with the sneaky, lowdown shit he would do like fucking with crackheads and prostitutes. I made a decision to put those fucked up ways behind me and never let them surface again. I wanted to be submissive and independent; but Derron didn't want that. He actually wanted a scarecrow female. That's what I call females who just stand there and allow a man to dominate them physical and mentally without using any of their own skills or making choices for themselves. On the other hand, I allowed Derron to dominate me both physically and emotionally, yet my mind was still my own. The key word here is "Allowed". I allowed Derrron to feel like he was controlling me, but actually it was the other way around. I read once in a book that if you allow a man to feel like he is in control, you'll actually be in control of him because that's how you get whatever you want out of your man. Those hoodrat chicks have no brains and I've always been an independent thinker and outgoing woman who made her own decisions and carried her own. Becoming passive was more of a choice for me, rather than a religion.

Derron one day told me again for the second time that we needed time apart for no perceptible reason. I didn't know if I had done something foul to him or what. I was hurt but at the same time curious as too what Derron was up to. He began to go MIA (missing in action) on a regular basis. I knew where to find him and I was afraid of him seeing me at the club of his choice and I knew that he would get pissed off. My insecurities began getting the best of me, and I was crying and feeling depressed almost everyday. No one was able to get through to me about him.

"Let that nigga go!" Belinda said, while listening to me sob on the phone. "Girl, I told you that motherfucker had hoes in different area codes and you… you already got a car out of him. Let it ride from now." Although, I listened to her I didn't agree with her especially about the car. I didn't want the damn car in the first place and even now so that I didn't have him anymore. I mean what's the point? He bought me a car, and then left me? Now that's a mental fuck-up for you. Nevertheless, Derron knew in his heart that I wouldn't disobey him so he roamed freely throughout every fucking club in College Park.

One evening Belinda called to check up on me. "What's up girl?" she said with a cheerful tone.

"Oh nothing … just lying down watching some TV right now," I replied in a down and out voice.

She laughed and said, "Seneca, girl get out on that depression shit. I know you're sitting home waiting for Derron to call, but you are a make-it-happen get results Aries bitch! So by nature you're supposed to snap out of this shit … Will you?" I started laughing because she always had a way of making me see the other side. I did the same thing for her and Vanessa. "Seneca I'm getting ready to go do a bachelor party in College Park. Do you want to come?" she asked. Belinda placed me on speakerphone while she dressed.

"Ah… I don't know girl. I wouldn't know what to do there," I said, making an uneasy expression with my face. "I guess I'll go, since I'm not doing anything else." I replied later.

We got off the phone and I got dressed and headed to Decatur to pick up Belinda. When I arrived she was waiting on the front porch. Looking like she had just stepped out of magazine, Belinda got into my car. "Girl, excuse the car," I said, looking at her to see her expression. "Ha, Ha, Now Sen... I known you ten years and nothing changed about your jungle ass car," she said as she tried to fit her bag in the back seat. We both laughed and began talking about what was going on with me and what was going out with her and her baby daddies. About twenty minutes later we arrived at an apartment complex where Belinda was going to be dancing. While pulling up to the door, I noticed several guys hanging around the front door. "Well ... we're here. Seneca, pop the trunk," Belinda said rushing out of the car. I jumped out too and grabbed some of her bags out of the trunk. Damn, my man would be pissed if he knew that I was at this type of party, I thought to myself as I closed the trunk.

When we walked into the house, there were guys sitting around everywhere drinking, smoking, getting lap dances and everything else. I been around some wild shit a time or two in my life, but I carried myself so much like a lady that people would often accuse me of trying to act like I was the better than them, or like I was a white girl. I was just being me. We headed to the bedroom upstairs where all the other dancers were getting dressed. The girls were pretty, some more than others. However, they were all there for the same purpose and that was to make money. I felt very out of place, but I made myself useful and helped Belinda get her dance outfits together.

It was time for her to go and entertain the guys downstairs in the party and I didn't want to stay up in the room so I decided to go to the bottom of the stairs to watch. As Belinda was performing, one guy came up to me and asked me why wasn't I dancing?

I told him that I wasn't a dancer and that I was there to support my girl. The longer I stayed the more I began to feel as if I didn't belong there. As I sat there I thought about Derron and where he could have been; who he was with and why the hell did I come here. You know those kind of mental mind fuck questions. I kept daydreaming so much and the questions kept running through my head I couldn't understand why I even came with her in the first place, because it wasn't like I was much help to her anyway.

I end up leaving Belinda at her party and my mind kept telling me to drive by this night-spot that Derron hung out at but he didn't allow me to hang out there. I decided to drive by the Ritz instead and saw his car parked in the VIP parking area. My heart raced faster than a person hitting the crack pipe. I was scared as hell because I knew I would get in trouble if he saw me in the club. Shaking like a leaf inside my car, I decided to take a chance and go in anyway. I was looking damn good in a fuchsia pink dress that Derron had ordered me never to wear again. As I entered the club, I walked quickly pass the first bar trying to disguise myself. Young niggas were trying to holler and pull on me from every side. I politely turned them down and continued to look for Derron. As I walked toward the second bar, my eyes met his eyes. Oh shit! I said muttered to myself. I tried to play it off by smiling and walking a little faster in my stilettos. As I got closer to the bar, I began slowing my pace.

"What the hell? This is not ... what I think it is," I said with a cracking voice. I stopped dead in my tracks, almost like I was a deer caught in headlights. I mean…I couldn't move. There my man was hugged up with some girl. Her back was turned toward me so I couldn't see her face, but I knew it wasn't anyone I knew. If it wasn't for the deputy sheriff in the club, I would have probably dragged her ass out of the club! I can't do that. That's not the woman you are today, I kept telling myself. It seemed as if my heart stopped beating and as if everyone around me was moving and talking in slow motion. I stood in front of Derron, while this girl's back was toward me and just stared at him. One single tear fell from my eye and I quickly wiped it away.

Derron whispered something in the girl's ear and came over to me. I said," Baby… Baby, is that your new girlfriend?" He said, "Uh, aw… I'm drunk I don't know what I'm doing."

"What are you doing?" I said, in a scared, fragile voice. He didn't answer, and then he walked back over to the girl and whispered something to her again. I was too afraid to approach him while he talked, so I waited until he walked off and then followed him towards the front door of the club. "We need to talk, we need to talk," I repeated over and over. When we got near the club entrances and he turned around and stopped. He began yelling at me, "What the fuck are you doing in here? What the fuck do you have on?!" He totally caught me off guard, because he flipped the strip on me so quickly that I didn't see it coming. My comeback words were, "Aw, Uh, I.... But, but baby …" As I looked around the club I thought. Can anyone sell me a vowel sound! I was totally lost for words. I felt like the dumbest chick in the club. I was so lost for words that Derron took the fear I displayed to him and ran with it.

Shortly after that, he left the club with me running behind him trying to explain myself. He tried to get in his car to leave and I stood between the door begging, pleading and crying. Some would probably ask why I was begging and pleading with him as if I was the one caught in the club. Shit, I'm still trying to figure that part out myself. Finally, he shoved me out of the way with his arm and drove off. I was distraught and in tears while onlookers stared in confusion and amazement. I ran to my car an in a panic and tried calling him several times, but he had turned off his phone.

Each time I called his phone the voicemail came on again: "Hey what's up everybody. My man Tupac said, only God can judge me… I like that." The words repeated over and over as I continued to call. Not giving a damn about anything at this time, I left hateful messages on his voicemail. I then decided to check his voicemail, but to my surprise he had changed the pass code. "Oh shit! He must have found out somehow that I knew his code," I said trying to figure out what I needed to do next. "What the hell his code could be?" I repeated over and over out loud in the car. 4455, 4545, 9876, 6789, or maybe it's the last four digits of his social security number. I contemplated in my head while dialing frantically. "I have to know if he is with that girl!" I cried out to myself once again in the car. The only way I could continue checking his voicemail was if he kept his phone turned off. So I had to calm down so that I could think rationally, and then I was able to mesh through the number to break the code. When I first started checking his messages I had been very good with this code-breaking thing, or God himself had just wanted me to know what was up with him. "Okay, I'm going to try one more time, then I'm just going home," I said to myself. "Please enter your pass code," the voicemail said. While biting my bottom lip very hard, I held my breath and pressed 4545. "That is pass code is incorrect," the voicemail said. 4455 was next number I tried, then I keyed in 9.8.7.6 and there was a short pause on the phone. "Fuck! I guess it wasn't meant for me to know," I said silently to myself, while taking the phone away from my ear. Just as I was getting ready to press the END button the voicemail said, "You have one new message." My heart skipped beats as if it was playing hopscotch. I listened to the voicemail literally holding my breath. "Hey Derron, This is Sheniqia. I'm waiting at the Shell gas station by 285," a young distorted female voice said. I quickly saved the messages as new, so that when he checked it, it would look as if the message was still unheard. After putting on some makeup and getting my emotions together I looked down at my watch while biting my nails then said, I gotta go to his house and talk to him. I felt no need to go by the gas station because it had been twenty minutes that I had been in sitting in my car in the parking lot of the club, and Derron had been gone for about thirty minutes now. So if he hadn't checked the voicemail chances are he hadn't met that girl there.

I left the club and since I had to pass the Shell gas station on my way to I-285, I drove by slowly just to see if his Cadillac was parked behind the building or something. Just like I thought, he wasn't there; neither did I see anyone waiting in a car. However, had she been there I wouldn't have confronted her because I didn't know her and my beef was with Derron, not her. When I arrived at his apartment on Love Joy Road, his car was parked in front and usually if he had company over, the parking space next to his car would be taken up. As I approached the door, I prayed a little and then I knocked. "Yeah, who is it?" Derron said not opening the door. "Baby it's me Seneca. Please let me in." He opened the door and start reading my ass like a book. "I told you it was over! Why the fuck did you come to my house! This is the shit that I don't have time for!" I was astounded and stuttered as I said, "But… but Derron please, please tell me what I did wrong? I've never cheated and I've always being submissive to you." He stood in the doorway giving me a dead stare, then said, "Well obviously you don't obey like you should, because first of all, you have on that skimpy ass dress that I told you **NOT** to wear! Then you came to my fucking club and to top it all off you came to my fucking house! How the fuck do you call that obeying… Uh! Uh!" With tears and makeup running down my face I pleaded, "Baby, please listen to me, I want to please you. I was only there because I went somewhere with Belinda, other than that I wouldn't have been there. You know this!" Derron took two steps back from the doorway and said, "Well, fuck it. You don fuck up with me. You need to leave because I'm going to call the police." I believed that he was threatening to call the police to get me to leave.

I turned away and left his house hurt, torn and in distress. It was officially certified Derron and I had truly broken up. I asked myself why, but to be honest about the situation, I hadn't a clue.

The next three months I went through straight hell, agony and confusion because I had no clue why he broke up with me. He did not want to see me, talk to me, or hear anything about me. He was spotted out at bars with females, but I still felt he loved me and that he was playing hard to get, just to stay in control. Every day was a struggle for me, and I was literally sick from having no contact with him. I would call and drive by his house just to see if he was home, though I was afraid to knock on the door, because of his harsh, nonchalant demeanor. The Christmas holiday season was creeping up and I went on with my life to some degree, doing the things that I had to do, like taking care of my girls, working, and barely eating. Every now and then I hung with my girlfriends.

One day while Christmas shopping at South Dekalb Mall I wanted to get him and his baby son that I loved so much something for Christmas. I decided to try my luck once again and call and to my surprise this time, he answered. I was flabbergasted and almost cried. "Hello Daddi, how are you?" I asked in a nervous, soft voice. Derron held the phone for a second before answering, "Nothin, what's up?" My voice cracked as I told him that I'd missed him so fucking much and that I had Christmas presents for him and his son. I asked him if I could bring them over and leave them on his doorstep. He agreed and I dropped the presents off at the door and left. I felt better because at least he'd accepted the gifts. He spent Christmas with his friends and I spent Christmas with my family, but of course I wanted nothing more than to be with him.

CHAPTER 11
LOSING ME TO BE LOVED BY HIM

It was the beginning of a new year, and things hadn't changed much in my life. I had made my New Years resolution to go forward with my modeling and acting career and not to let anyone distract me. I was determined to this time. The only thing is that I was trying to go on with my life but Derron still owned my heart.

It was the ninth of January before Derron and I finally talked on the phone again. The conversation was full of emotions, deep breathing, and silence all at the same time. Neither, one of us wanted to say I miss you first. So we continued just listening to each other breathe. However, I could tell that we both still felt one another very deeply. I finally gave in and asked him if I could come over and he said yes. I was excited and nervous but I jumped right in the shower and got dressed because I was anxious to get over there. "He's really allowing me to come over." I said to myself getting dressed in the mirror. I just had to tell someone so I called Vanessa and Belinda on a three-way call. First i called Belinda and told her that I had something to tell her and Ness together. I asked her to call Nessa on her three-way, so she did. Belinda kept insisting that I tell her but I felt a need to tell both of them at the same time. When we finally got Nessa on the phone and Belinda was screaming for me to tell her. "What is it? What is it Seneca?" she said. "Did you get breast implants" Did you meet L.L.Cool J?" I interrupted her and told her to calm her ass down. Vanessa was on the phone and now Belinda had her all excited about my news that she didn't even know. "Guess what?" I said to them in an excited voice. "Girl, ain't nobody got time to be damn guessing…

just tell us!" Belinda shouted. "I'm going over to my Daddi's house!" I screamed. Belinda yelled out, "You are what! Are you fucking stupid? You know he ain't any good so don't ever say that I didn't warn you if you get hurt again!" Rolling my eyes while holding the phone I said to myself I don't want to hear it… la, la, la. Vanessa didn't have much to say about it. She had the "Whatever makes you happy" attitude. After talking to them I mentioned that I needed to get ready to leave because he was expecting me shortly. As I was hanging up the phone I heard Belinda mumble a smart remark but I was so not trying to hear it and just proceeded to hang up the phone.

At 8:10 p.m that evening, I arrived at Derron's house and even more nervous and anxious than ever. When I knocked on the door Derron yelled out, "It's open." I walked into the living room where he was watching basketball. I came in and kissed him very softly on his lips. After I kissed him, I sat down next to him on the sofa and got comfortable.

I was quite insecure about how he felt about me since we had been apart for 3 months. I wanted to get a feel for his vibe before giving him some long overdue affection and sex. His split personality made me approach him with caution. At times, I couldn't tell if Derron was going, coming or really being sincere about his feelings. He simply had my head so fucked that if he told me to jump, I would sit because I would have thought that it was a test. His stupid ass tests were to discover what he needed to find out without even asking you a question. He expected me to know what to do, what not to do, when to speak and when not to speak. I was no mind reader, and neither his tests, nor his punishments were something I could deal with. As Derron continued watching basketball and smoking his blunt he put his hand on my legs and began caressing my thigh. He moved his hand up and down my legs and then went between them and into my panties. This was the sign that I had been looking for that gave me a green light that said, "GO". I heeded every move he was making on me and then I followed his lead. The foreplay made us both crave each other more intensely than the first time we had met. Maybe it was because I had practice abstinence while I waited for him. Derron molest me silently throughout the evening. He did not saying a word but his nature said it all. It stood straight up from the sweat pants that he was wearing as if his dick was a compass that pointed straight towards his bedroom. Enough said, I followed his arrow in the direction in which it pointed. It then led me to the bedroom. I smirked and had serene memories of us while getting undressed. "I'll be right back. Go ahead in lie down," Derron said as he left the room to go get something. When he returned he had a cup of beer in his hand and he began taking off his pants. I really wanted to discuss our relationship but I figured that it could wait until after we made love. We began kissing each other feverishly. The passion, lust and desire continued to grow rapidly. There was nothing between us but opportunity and air. We went for it, leaving nothing to chance with an abundance of sucking, licking and partaking every inch of one another's body and suffocating our private parts by pressing them tightly together. The sweat increased on our bodies and we could only hear the sound of clapping our bodies made together harder.

We must have went at it for about 2 straight hours before Derron suddenly introduced me to his new freaky side, or perhaps it was an old hidden freaky side that was already apart of him and he had never let me know about. Though I was curious I didn't inquire about it. I just went along with the flow of things to find out what was up with this new liking. As I began performing oral sex on him I held his dick in one hand stroking it as I laid flat on my stomach and between his legs while he rested on his back. Abruptly, he grabbed my hand and began guiding it underneath him towards his ass. It felt weird doing so, because it's not like it was a part of our normal routine of foreplay – or any other play. I indulged him trying to see where he was going to go with it, so I placed my hand on his ass and to be quite honest… that was about it for me. I knew not to fuck with a black man's ass, not even for play. I thought to myself that my man is the hardest thug I've ever seen, so I know for sure not to try him like that. Derron began to push my hand up between his ass cheeks and then he grabbed my middle finger to direct it towards his exit door. "Naw, I must be imagining things. Of course, he made an honest error," I thought silently. So I proceeded in giving oral pleasure to my man and moved my hand once more off of his ass. Again for the second time, Derron grabbed and directed my middle finger into his ass and I held it there. I was in a state of confusion not knowing what the fuck was going on with him but I dared not to say. I paused for a second from giving him oral pleasure to peek up at him. His eyes were closed and his head was tilted back as if he was ready for me to proceed and he was ready to receive. While he still had his eyes closed. I stared up at him and imagined Scooby Doo saying to him, "What da you want me to do?" then I smirked and began to indulged him with my index finger just as he wanted me to do. This was a turn on for him, but new for me. I felt confused because he really liked this shit. In all my life I have never had a black man, or any man for that matter wanting me to do such a thing to his ass. After it was over, Derron did his usual cigarette break.

Derron's fantasies began to play out every single time we had sex. I knew in my mind something wasn't right with this shit but in my heart I loved this man and I kept telling myself that he was a thug. "No fucking way could my man be ... gay!" I sighed over and over. 2 months had passed and I needed to confide in someone about this finger in ass ordeal with Derron. "Who should I talk to? Should it be Belinda and Vanessa," I said while looking through my contacts on my cellphone. Belinda would talk shit and make jokes about it, but Vanessa ... well shit she can't hold water, but she won't laugh in my face about it either." I pondered. I ended up calling Vanessa and told her about this new found encounter with Derron. She swore she wouldn't tell anyone. I told her that no one knew except for her and if it got out about my busines, I will know that she had to have been the one to tell it. She advised me to go to a place called, Starships that sells sex toys and buy a dildo to try it on him to see how he would respond. I was already scared to try him like that although he had allowed and wanted me to penetrate him with my finger. I detested going into those places because it seemed as if everyone there knew that you were going to have sex. I headed to Starship one day after work and bough a small dildo and some anal bead. Then I went straight over to his house. I placed the dildo in a brown paper bag and then went to pick up some hot wings, blue cheese and celery for him to eat. After finishing his wings he washed up and we began having sex. After Derron had came I decided to get ready to start the test, but I was nerve as hell. "Um... Baby, I'll be right back," I whispered as I got up out of bed to go to the restroom. When I returned to the bedroom Derron was lying on his stomach listening to the quiet Storm on the V103 radio station. The lyric played as Derron sanged, "Let me tell how much I love you, let me tell how much I need you. Make it last forever…" Our song was playing on the radio and I began humming the song out loud. "That's our song, ain't it baby," Derron said moving his foot to the music. I smirked and said, "Yep, baby that's it." I went to the loveseat where my brown bag was lying. Carefully watching him I went inside my purse while he was still lying on his stomach. As I was walking back over towards the bed I could hear my heart rate speeding up. Derron didn't turn over but asked me what I was doing. Speaking softly, I answered "Oh nothing baby, I'm getting something out of my purse that's all." I didn't know how he was going to respond and I was actually hoping that this would be the time that he was going to knock my ass the fuck out for trying him like this. I went over to the bed and started off rubbing the dildo on his ass just to see if he would turn over in curiousity to see what I was rubbing on him but he didn't, so I proceeded further with my course of action. Finally I got up an enough to nerves to push it in. At first, I went slowly to see how he would react and then I just plunged it up in ass. I was astounded, because Derron didn't even make a sound, but I could tell that he was really comfortable with it and liked it because he continued to spread his legs further apart. I kept trying to see his facial expressions, but he didn't make any. He was taking the dildo with the greatest of ease so I pushed it even further. I was screwing him with this dildo and as if he was screwing me with his dick! At the same time I was screaming on the inside but continued plunging it until I got a response. After at least 10 minutes of fucking him, he suddenly responded with a delayed reaction. "Ouch, baby that hurts take it out." he muttered. By that time, he had already been indicted and found guilty of liking to having his ass fucked with. I then got up and went into the bathroom and locked the door behind me. I turned on the shower just to let him think that I was getting ready to get in. I just sat on the toilet and thought to myself, "Please tell me my man isn't a homo-thug! This got to a dream or something." I shook my head in disbelief. It's probably a fad or something and then I answered myself saying, "Hell naw! Real men won't allow you to do this kind of shit to them … would they? The man that I love is ga-. No! No! This just can't be real" I whispered. Derron knocked on the door and yelled out, "Baby, did you say something?" tapping on the door. I got scared and thought that he over heard me and quickly made of something.

"Umm..Just singing Daddi," I shouted over the running water, then I began singing just to play it off, "Make it last forever, and ever and ever." I heard Derron laughing out loud and then he walked away from the door. I didn't want to believe what I had just experienced, but it was the rawest reality that I had ever encountered. I wanted to deny it all, so I looked around the bathroom at his Swiss Army and Curves cologne, then I looked at facial shaver. I even looked at the toilet paper to see if there were any pretty prints on them, but founded nothing that might indicated that he was gay. Sighing with relief, I told myself that maybe guys today like this kind of stuff now. I pulled myself back together and flushed my emotions about that situation down the toilet and went back into the bedroom. Derron was getting dressed to leave and go somewhere. "You alright?" he asked. I smiled and nodded my head, then got back on the bed. "I'll be back, I'm going to pick up a bag of weed up the street," he said rushing out. "Oh... ok then," I said putting on one of his t-shirts. When he returned I had fell asleep and he woke me up to let me know that he was back.

The next morning I was quiet and still in disbelief and confusion about my man. He got up being his normal self. I fixed him a peanut butter sandwich and gave him the vitamin that he took every morning. I couldn't let him know that I felt awkward about what had happened the night before, so I played it off by kissing him before leaving to head to work. In my mind, I was saying that I would never fuck with him again and everything continued replaying in head.

Later on the day, he called me around lunchtime and I was still kind of quiet and nonchalant. He asked, "Why are you so quiet, Seneca?" I told him there was no reason. He then said, "I hope you don't think anything strange about last night just because I got a little freaky with you."

I quickly responded back and said, "Oh no daddi, I hadn't even thought about it again." Then we changed subjects and after about ten minutes we hung up. I had made up in my mind to break up with him because the reality part of this kept telling me that it was a gay act, no matter how much he tried to convince me otherwise. The love I had for him made me struggle with not leaving and what was morally right. After hours of debating with myself, I once again deny the facts and decided to stay with this man that I in love with. I reflected on his swagger, hardness and masculine side to stay focus on him. I continued telling myself that he was a thug.

This sexual custom became the norm every time we had sex. Although I knew this went against every thing I stood for in my heart. As a woman, his woman there was still a part of me that wanted to please him so I dealt with it even if it meant doing this finger thing to him. I don't want to lose him again because we had just got back together. Each day I looked for ways to remind me that my man was a full-fledged thug. "He has Long braids, Curve cologne, Sagging pants, Newport cigarettes, Corona, deep voice." I repeated over and over in my head every time the thought of him being down-low or gay crossed my mind. I convinced myself of it and pretended he was just open and different from other thugs. It got to the point that when he had sex with me his dick would get only semi-hard. It was sad to say that if I wasn't plunging a finger in his ass; his dick was going to remain polish sausage hard and limp. The year was passing and the deeper we became into this abnormal sex but during the time I was just fingering him in his ass and I still couldn't find anything normal about this sexual relationship. Derron became so used to me doing this act to him that when it came to just trying to have typical sex, there was no chance of it. That's when it really started affecting me and reality kicked in and showed me that it was no longer me that he was truly attracted to, but the act I performed on him. Reality was forcing me out of denial. But the love I had for him also kept me foolish. Even when it continued to happen over and over, I would try to lie to myself each time by saying that our sex life was just extraordinary. It began to remind of the dream I had when I first met him. I then knew that even though I was living a sinful life, God was still trying to reveal things to me about him but I couldn't see it clearly because my eyes were wide shut.

Derron continued living a somewhat-thug lifestyle dealing with hoodrat girls and hanging out with his boys, but that's what he threw me off about his sexuality. I knew he was dealing with females because I continue listening to his voicemail messages. Often, I would just play the dumb fox role which required me to suppress my emotions and go with the flow. Pretending that what I heard on the phone never happened, or if it had already happened it was just a fuck thing. Derron would sometimes call me when I was out and ask me where I was. I would mess with his head and say, "Oh, I'm downtown with Camilla." I would use the name of a girl that I had heard on his voicemail. Of course, it was someone he knew or had been with. Derron would go almost silent on the phone like he was under a spell or something. I knew this fucked with him every time, and I played it off so well, but it was still unbelievable that he never second-guessed it. This game went on and on for several months until I became accustomed and numb to it. He continued with his want to be mack daddy act and I went along with it. He felt he was ahead of me, but in reality I was two steps ahead of him.

Finally, I discovered that it wasn't a game after all. I was losing myself in his masquerade. Although I put up with it went along with, and stuck out with the relationship, I was very alert to what was happening to my self-esteem and self worth. Things that I have never put up with in my life seemed to be staring me right in the face. As my mother once said, "Child, you traded the witch for the devil." I was again experiencing abuse, just on a different level and with a different man, or as Whitney Houston would sing it "Same script, different cast." You see, no matter how good the grass felt on the other side, I now believed that it was only turf. It was superficial and artificial. He is a hard thug with a silver tongue. Who wore Curves cologne and had big dick and townhouse apartment that he called, Home.

CHAPTER 12
THE PORCH LIGHT CAME ON

I continued the submissive role towards Derron and he really put me under conditions and limited restrictions. I wasn't allowed to go to the same club he hung out at unless he said it was ok. After so many times of asking if I could go out with him. Derron finally decided to allow me to accompany him and his friend Kenar to the club. He was finally allowing me to hang out with him in his forbidden place. We got dressed and head to club. I'd never hung out so much at clubs until I met Derron.

When we arrived I was looking pretty sexy in my pink dress and Derron wore his usual gear, a big T-shirt and Macavelli jeans. I didn't drink so Derron and Kenar were doing all the drinking. As we cruised through the club Kenar went to the dance floor, while Derron and I walked around the club holding hands. We finally decided to station ourselves on a wall by the entrance. I was standing in front of my 6 foot 7 thug when two young hoodrats came and stood directly beside me. I didn't think much of it until one of the girls said to her friend, "Hey, you see that guy right there, he can't fuck," Since they were standing right beside me and pointing up to Derron I assumed she was talking about him. The girl said again, "That guy right there?" and this time I didn't take my eyes of her and confirmed that she was speaking about my man. I didn't say anything to her for two reasons. One of the reasons was that I felt that she was saying that to try to get to me and the seond reason was that they were just some hater females who were jealous that I was there with him. She and her friend started laughing and walked away. It was obvious that she wanted me to respond, but it didn't faze me so I mentally kept it moving. Derron asked me, "Baby, what did they say," I smirked and sighed, "They said you couldn't fuck baby. They said you couldn't fuck." He said in a heated tone, "I don't even know that girl and ain't never fucked her!" I told him that it was cool and I didn't care if he had fucked her or not. I also told Derron that I didn't think she would randomly pick him out of a 100 hundred men in the club and I didn't care! As Derron continued to huff and puff about the girl, I danced in front of him. He then told me that he was going to confront her if he saw her again. He grabbed my hand and we began walking through the club and went into the pool room. As we walked through the pool room I spotted the hoodrats who had made the allegations against my so-called faithful thug. I told him there was the girls that said made the statements. Before I knew it, he snapped on them. Derron yelled out to the light skinned girls, "Hey, did you say something to me?" The one of the girls answered in a timid voice, "Uh *No, I did not*." As we passed the pool table and was making our way to the exit of the pool room, one of the girls yelled from behind us, "Yeah, nigga, I said something! I probably said you couldn't fuck!" Derron let man hand go and started walking back towards her and then he replied, "How do you know, bitch! Did I fuck you?!" Derron and this one girl were arguing back and forth with me in between them. I kept yelling for him to come on and let it go but he wouldn't listen. The girls did not make any eye or word gestures toward me at all, they were totally after his ass. I didn't have a problem with standing up for him, but I would have looked pretty stupid running up on somebody that could be telling the truth about the situation and get my face fucked up because of his shit. I was smarter than that and besides it didn't faze me one bit what they had said. I led Derron out of the pool room and that's when one of the girls yelled out, "Yeah nigga… that's why you like dick up your ass!" I took a hard swallow, but it seemed as if something was caught in my throat. I stopped dead in my tracks and took a deep breath and pretend like I didn't hear her say that. The more I tried to ignore it the words kept replaying in head in slow motion, "Dick up your ass" … cow bells, whistles, sirens, light bulbs blowing out and everything else was going off in my head! For a quick second, I had a visual flashback of recalling the new sexual experience that Derron had introduced me to back in January. Derron, did not respond to the comment; he walked fast and silent as he could out the door and never even turned around. While I stood there frozen as I thought about going back to ask the girl what she meant by that. I was scared too, because although Derron had walked off, Kenar was standing right at the exit waiting for me. Since they were hood girls, I felt that might take it well about me questioning her about my man. I charged it to the game and ran to catch up with Derron.

Once we arrived in the parking lot he started cussing me out, or just talking real loud and harsh to me as if I had done something wrong. He finally said, "Why didn't you beat her ass? I got to fight the men and the women!"

I answered, "I'm 33 years old with 3 kids what the hell do I look like fighting some rodent in a club?" All the way home Derron yelled and screamed about the same old scenario until he tired himself out. When we arrived at the house Derron stormed out of the car and went to bed. Shortly after, I got into bed and tried to comfort him, but Derron moved closer to the edge of the other side of the bed. He showed me that he was cold and distant so I didn't bother trying to deal with him for the rest of that night.

At about 3 o'clock in the morning, I woke up and found Derron missing from bed. In the pitch black of the room I smelled his cigarette burning, and then I looked out the bedroom door and towards the living room and saw one tiny red light coming from the sofa area. Derron had waked up to go smoke a cigarette and was obviously thinking about the incident while sitting in the dark.

The next morning we got up and talked and I explained that I wasn't scared but I wasn't getting into a fight with anyone. He protested his case, saying that I was supposed to have his back and that I should be down with him no matter what. I eventually gave in and like always, ended up apologizing for something I hadn't done. He swore that he would never take me to one of his clubs again. He made me feel as if it was my fault that that girl went off on him. "Had you never been there with me, all of this wouldn't have happened," he said looking down at his scratch lottery ticket that he had won $50 on the night before. "Yeah, you're right baby, and I sorry about that. I never want you to be hurt or embarrassed," I said to him. There was never any mention of the "dick in the ass" remark. We then went to have some make up sex and lay up. After a few hours, I gathered my things and hit I-285 to head home. As I was driving, I thought more and more about what the girl had said the night before. Derron's response had pretty much put my mind in an uproar and I was wondering what had really happened between them and had he really took some dick up the ass. I kept telling myself that I should have asked her what she meant by that and if she meant that he had been literally fucked by a dick or a dildo. I felt perhaps that I could have talked to her had I gone back into the club after Derron and Kenar had left. Like I said earlier, the light bulb had come on in my head about the situation and it never went off. I continued to scrutinize the issue of Derron and the dildo and I was not about to let it go. On the same token, I loved him and I wasn't going to leave my man without having a substantial amount of evidence proving that he was bisexual, gay or down-low, or which ever came f i   r   s   t.

CHAPTER 13
ONLY LADY IN THE HOUSE

Derron's birthday was coming up and this year was going to be the first time that I spent his birthday with him. I was excited and trying to plan something very special for him, despite all of the craziness that had happened between us the last two months. Derron was quite insecure about getting older. Everything that was use to insignificant mattered to him a little more now. He was concerned about his body, his looks, his age, his future, his friends and more important, our future. I was somewhat happy and had put in the far, far back of my mind the possibility that could be Derron gay or bisexual. Although those experiences with him became more and more regular every time we had sex. It had even got to the point where his dick wouldn't get hard unless I was fingering him in his ass. I dealt with it because I did not want to be without him. I just wrote off Derron as **NOT GAY,** just **FREAKY.** That means that he was guilty, but with explanation and therefore it wouldn't be held against him. Derron decided at the last moment that he just wanted to have his party at the club with his friends. I thought it was a great idea and I told him to invite all his girl and guy friends. I was excited because this would be the first time that I would meet all his female friends and they would have the opportunity to see the fine, sophiscated lady in his life. I figured that whoever these so called female were they were going to be a part of his life so I might as well get used to it. I called Vanessa and invited her to the meet us at the club.

Derron and I got dressed the evening of his birthday and headed to the club to wait for his friends to show up. One by one his guy friends started promenading into the club. They shook his hand and wished him a happy birthday as some of them also hugged and said hello to me. I sat down out of the way to let him socialize with his guy friends, and anticipated the arrival of the females. "Damn, it seems like none of the females are going to show," I said to myself. I went to ask Derron if he had invited his some female friends. He told me that he had invited them, but my gut was telling me different. Vanessa and one of her friends finally arrived, so I kicked it with them for a while, but it wasn't for long because Derron wanted me under him. Derron seemed to be having a great time at his gathering and I continued to buy him his favorite drinks like Corona, Long Island Iced Teas and Hennessey. After making sure that he was taking care of, I went to sit down and listen to the music. One of his friends came over to talk to me while Derron was talking to his other friend and when Derron noticed he got up and came on, and then grabbed my hand to pull me closer to him. I laughed on the inside because I saw that Derron was getting a bit jealous and insecure. However, I thought it was cute at the same time.

I excused myself to go to the restroom because I was feeling sick to my stomach. When I got into the restroom stall, I began vomiting. I was sick, but I was not going to let Derron know that because I didn't want to spoil his party. While sitting in the stall; my phone began to ring. It was Derron calling so I answered, "Hey Daddi," "Where are you? Are you okay?" he asked in a apprehensive tone. In a pepped up voice I answered, "Yes Daddi. I'm ok. I'm on my way out." I soon as I hung up the phone I ran out of the restroom and wash my face. I began remembering the time when Derron busted into the ladies restroom because I stayed in 20 minutes. Women were pulling up their pantyhose, doing their hair, and talking and he didn't care. I did not want it to happen again, so I sprinted out like Flo Jo and went back to the dance floor where he was standing. When I returned he asked me again if I was okay. I told him everything was fine and then I asked him had any of his female friends arrived. He told me no and started rubbing on my ass. I looked around and his 12 male friends were still hanging out. Under my breath I said, "What the hell is up with this shit. I'm not the only female here at his gathering?" On the outside I continued smiling and talking to Derron until one of his friend needed to speak to him privately. Derron excused himself and

I went to the DJ booth to ask him to give a shout out for Derron birthday. As I was walking toward the DJ booth I spotted another one of Derron's friend, Kenar coming in the club. After speaking with the DJ; I returned to Derron and we went started dancing. All of sudden, I started feeling sick again. "Damn, baby what wro…" I heard Derron saying as I raced back to restroom once again. I must have stayed in the restroom for about ten minutes and this time Derron didn't call me on my cellphone, so I really took that as a sign that he was heading to the restroom. After throwing up for the second time, I walked as fast as I could up the breezeway to get back to my man but when I returned I notice Kenar and Derron talking alone, so I went to sit back down at the table. Derron turned around and notice that I was back from the restroom and came over. Kenar looked over at me and I waved my hand and he didn't speak and then he went to seat at the bar alone. This was totally unusual because every time I saw the guy he was happy and had so much energy, especially if we were at a club.

I asked Derron what was wrong with Kenar and he said he didn't know and shortly after that Kenar left the club without saying goodbye. I thought it was very strange and for the life of me I couldn't figure out what had happened between Kenar and Derron.

As it turned out, I was the only female who showed up at my man's party. When the party was over and everyone was leaving; the DJ finally decided to give the shout out that I requested earlier. "A special young lady wants to give a birthday shout-out to her man, Derrrrronnn who in the house. Happy Birthday, Happy Birthdayyyyy" When Derron heard the shout out he began smiling and asked me did I do that. I nodded my head and put began laughing. He then thanked me and said good looking out that is some good shit. After everyone had left, Derron and I left went to the car to go to his house. While driving, out of the blue he asked me if I was pregnant. I answered very slowly, "Uh…noooo Daddi. Why did you ask me that?" I asked. He then told me if you were, I could tell him. Again, I replied no, but deep inside I realized it was a possibility. So I told him I didn't want to talk about it anymore and I just wanted to enjoy the evening with him. When we arrive home, we made passionate love as usual. Being on the outside looking into my life, you would have thought I had it going on. I was spending every night of the week with him and our life was somewhat grand. We had small problems but for the most part, we were happy. At least, I was and I never looked back on our past issues. We had haters trying to interrupt our master plan, but nothing could come between the two of us, except for...

CHAPTER 14
THREE LIVES TO SHARE, BUT ONLY ONE TO BEAR

I finally was experiencing what I thought was true happiness. There were many pros and cons, but it was still a new feeling I had never felt before. It seems as if his world and mine was truly combined. We got up on the weekends and went to the mall to shop. He bought his favorite Macaveli jeans and Tupac gear, and I bought my stilettos.

One day we drove to the mall and I became nauseated. Derron turned to me and said, "That's it baby, you are taking a pregnancy test and I'm going to buy it!" I looked at him and said, "Baby what are you talking about. I'm not pregnant!" He stared down at me and said, "Seneca, I hope you're not lying to me," and he grabbed my hand and we continued shopping and walking through the mall. On our way back to his house Derron said that he was going to stop by the drug store to get a pregnancy test. I told him that promised that I would take a teste the following week. The next day which was Sunday morning, I got up and fixed him his regular peanut butter sandwich. We were getting ready to go to church and usually I would stay with him the all weekend and go home that evening. However the only thing that was different about this Sunday is that I woke up and immediately had to rush to the restroom to throw up. His radar went sky high. He jumped up out of bed and came into the restroom yelling, "You are pregnant!" Bent over the toilet on my knees I gathered breath to tell him again that i wasn't. "Well how come you throwing up all over the damn place then?" he asked with an anger tone. He then proceeded to walk out of the restroom scratching his balls and yelled out that I better make sure you get that pregnancy test or else I was going to have to answer to him. When he said that I managed to look up at him and the look on his face told me that he was serious as hell. I hesitated before responding, "Okay fine, whatever you say Daddi."

The days turned into weeks, and weeks turned into a month. I still hadn't attempted take a pregnancy test. Almost every day Derron would ask me to go and buy a test and I would make up an excuse about not having the money to get it. I had my issues of being uncertain about what I would do if I were pregnant and I felt Derron wouldn't be too pleased. He made me feel that it was all my responsibility and I should take precaution when it came to us having sex and me not getting pregnant. This is the man I loved and I wanted more than anything to have his baby, but he spoke so harshly about it that I was afraid to tell him how I felt. One day at work I decided to take a pregnancy test just to see what the results would be and I would let him know later on… maybe. During lunch, I went to the restroom but I mentioned to Donna, my co-worker who worked in radio that I was planning to take a pregnancy test. She told me to let her know the result as soon as I knew. I went into the bathroom stall and sat on the toilet; my heart was beating so damn fast. I started urinating on the little stick and waited anxiously for the results, but at the same time I thought about what Derron. I thought to myself, maybe he'll surprise me and want me to keep it, and my second thought was he's going to hit the roof! Either way, I had to wait the three longest minutes of my life just to find out. The results were finally in and the only thing I had to do was look, but I was afraid to. I could toss the test in the garbage and never even bother looking at it or face the music. I slowly picked up the test with my eyes shut. One by one I opened my eyes to see the results and there were two lines in the little window. I picked up the box and read the side panel. It read one line … not pregnant; two lines … pregnant. I was speechless. "Oh my God …two lines," I said, as I sat down on the toilet seat. "Shit that means I'm really and truly pregnant," I whispered looking down at the floor. My first response was excitement, and then I thought about how I was going to tell Derron. I rubbed my stomach and said, "I'm having Derron's son." At least I was hoping because I had already had three girls and lord knows I couldn't handle another girl.

It was time for me to go back to my desk, so I wiped myself and pulled up my panties, washed my hand and then left out the restroom.

I met Donna in the hallway when she was on her way to the restroom to check on me. When she looked at me, she had this wide eye grin on her face. I looked at her and just nodded yes." are you going to do?" she said. I didn't answer her because I didn't know myself, and besides I didn't know what Derron was going to say. Donna shook her head and then she started reminding me of everything I'd told her about Derron and the way in which he treated me. Immediately I interrupted her and I said, "Hold up girl! I remember what I told you about this nigga of mine but shit right now I don't need a reminder." I then caught myself and apologized because she was just concerned about me. In fact I noticed that I had begun snapping on anyone who said anything negative about him. Donna said she just wanted me to make to right decision for my life with everything in mind.

It was just about 3:00 pm and Derron called me at my desk. "How's your day going?" he asked. "Fine" I said in a very soft voice. He then said, "Baby, are you alright?" I told him that I wasn't feeling well. I guess I was trying to set to stage and lead up to telling him that I was pregnant. Derron was always on top of things and smart to the degree that it was hard to try and pull anything over on him. He asked me again did I take a pregnancy test." I stuttered and answered, "N-Not yet baby," and advised him I would take it after I got off of work that day. He said okay and we hung up. All that time afterwards I was thinking of ways to break the news to him. I called Vanessa and told her about it. She was so excited and that made me happy, but then the reality kicked in again. Derron was going to snap! I kept telling myself that he might want it, but maybe he won't. My mind kept racing back and forth and I had no peace at all. My cousin told me to tell him and assured me that he would probably want me to have it. It was almost 4:45 and I had not got much work done when Derron called. This time I told him I would call him back when I got off. I was stalling for time because I wanted to consult with more friends about the situation. I discussed the situation with relatives, friends, co-workers, strangers, pastors and prayer hotlines. No one could give me the answer that would comfort me in my time of need before I spoke with him.

Around 7:30 that night I finally called him back and he said in a very calm, deep voice, "So… what is it? Are you pregnant?" I hesitated and said,"Uh, uh… yes". First there was total silence on the phone, and then he said in a loud, deep voice, "Uh … you know I'm going to leave you if you have that baby… right!" I stuttered and said, "But… but Derron I didn't say anything about having it." He was so serious that I could hear him breathing through the phone like a fierce animal. I was really scared to speak my mind now, so I sat quietly on the phone and listened to him tell me the thousands of reasons why I shouldn't have the baby. He made sure I knew he was serious about leaving and he wasn't listening to any thing I had to say. I almost forgot about being submissive to him and did not talk back, although I wanted to say, "Motherfucker, who the hell do you think you are!!" I didn't say anything and I sat in traffic in my car letting my silent tears speak for me. However, I couldn't let him know that I was crying, because crying in his eyes was a sign of weakness and he would only yell more and hang up in my face. Derron possessed hardness about himself like a probation officer, a judge, or a corrector. It was almost as if he felt he was God and I had to kneel down to worship and obey him. Nothing he did or said made me really snap on him because I had such a fear of losing him. We ended our conversation with the understanding that I was not going to keep the baby and the only evil fucker that was happy about that shit was Satan himself. Derron couldn't have given a damn about how I felt. He had shown me that he was becoming a very selfish son of a bitch, and his motto was to let me know that it was all about him … end of story. Then again, perhaps he had always been that selfish son of a bitch, and I just hadn't noticed it until now.

As the days went by we spoke about the pregnancy and even continued to have sex week by week. About two and a half months into the pregnancy he became really distant and so fucking cold that you could have frozen icicles on his dick. The secondo week in June, Derron's family was coming into town and he kept telling me to stay away because he needed to spend time with them. I believe it was just so he could continue to do his dirty work and I to hide that I was pregnant. Every time I called his phone he wouldn't answer, or if he answered he would just hold the phone. He was actually being so disrespectful that I went off on him like I have never ever done before. Here I was pregnant, alone and full of emotions. He just didn't realize that he was provoking an explosion to happen. Although I had sworn that I would never argue with another man and for that reason Derron had a bad habit of underestimating me because of my size. Often, he would refer to me as scary and fragile. "You're a white girl in black girl body," he would said shaking his head down at me. He was used to dealing with those hoodrat chicks who would use to cuss his ass out on the norm, and then they would go pick up him a thing of buffalo wings and a forty ounce of Ice Bud in the same hour. I guess I didn't quite fit that bill but I was a long way from being a punk bitch! He just didn't know it.

After so many endless days and nights of trying to contact hi; I finally snapped on him so hard that I'm sure he was surprised because he had never seen that side of me before. I use to always warn him to never underestimate the strength of someone who is small, and my hormones were kick boxing inside me. When I finally caught up with him, I was so mad with him that I said everything I even thought about saying in the past. I choked up enough courage to mention the finger in the asss thing. "Derron are you bisexual or gay?" I asked him in an angry, eagered voice. Derron held the phone for a second then answered, "If I am, or if I was you would still want me." At this time, I so pissed off and stunned by his answer that I forgot what I was going to say next. Usually, if I was going to tell him off about something but didn't have the nerve to do so, I would write it all down on paper: {Dear Motherfucker, dick in the booty, fudge packer wacker, son of a bitch. I can't stand you!} I would read it out loud in the mirror, then tear up the paper. After Derron said that he hung up the phone. I sat in my bedroom with the phone still to my ear listening to the automatic operator on the phone say, "If you are trying to make call; please dial the area code and the seven dighit number." The answer he gave then dawn on me. I began repeating it out loud trying to make sense of the phase. "If I was… you would still want me." I heard it over and over in my head. "What the hell is that supposed to mean? I simply asked for a Yes or No answer! Yes or fucking … No!" I muttered.

I sat there thinking to myself, He's probably right but I was still lit and pissed off by the statement. "Well I'm not sure what I'm going to do now that I'm in this mess alone. Should I keep it or should I have an abortion? I debated. I know when my friend Tessa went through this and they said she had to be at least twelve weeks before they would see her," I whispered as I picked up the yellow pages of the floor. "I couldn't possibly have an abortion. "I...I might die or something. I just can't go through it!" I cried. A little voice inside of my head said, Seneca you never know what might happen at least check it out. I opened the yellow pages and turn to the page with the read ABORTION written right at the top of the page. I also saw the word ADOPTION on the next page I flipped over. "I'll get some numbers for later, just in case I made up my mind" I said, writing the numbers down in my contact book and giving a big sigh. I begin to dial one of the numbers that I found in the yellow pages. The began to ring and a lady answered the phone, "Hello, It's a great day at Uprise Women Center. This is Cara, may I help you?" At first I held the phone because I wasn't sure about go.ing through with it, then I said, "Umm... hello. I just want to know how much it cost to have an abortion." The lady start out explaining to me that it depends on the amount of weeks I were and asked me If I had insurance. "Yes maam, I have Blue cross- Blue shield HMO" I replied. She asked to hold on for a moment then she came back and told me that the cost would be $250.00. I yelled, "$250.00. Why the hell do I have insurance then if it's going to still cost that much!" The told me that even with insurance I had to pay a percentage, then she advise me to call back if I had any other questions. I hung the phone and got back in bed and balded up rubbing my stomach. While laying in the bed I looked up towards the ceiling and said, "I would have never thought that I would be pregnant with Derron's son." I was hoping that if I had ever got pregnant by him that I would have a son.

One night during basketball season Derron went to his friend's house to watch the basketball game and leaving me behind as usual. My stomach started hurting and I begin to have vaginal bleeding. I got so worried that I thought that I could be having a miscarriage. I had already made up ten percent of my mind to have an abortion, mainly because of Derron's attitude towards me and I couldn't mentally handle the emotional abuse that he was dishing out. I think that was mainly the reason for the stomach pain and bleeding. "I should go the the hospital, but I was just talking about an abortion and now I'm concerned that I could be losing it!" I groaned with confusion. Since I was having vaginal bleedng I decided to the emergency room. I figured that I might as well call Derron to let him know, but first I needed to find someone to take me to the hopsital so I call Nessa and there was

no answer. I then try Belinda, then Neen, and finally Lynn and with no success. "Oh well, I'll take myself," I said. I grabbed my purse and car keys and began walking down the stairway from my third floor apartment when an extremely hard pain hit me in my lower vaginal and bikini area. "Whoa... Oh Shit!" I said in a panic and then I braced myself to sit down on the stairs. After sitting there for a second I got up and made it down to the second floor stairway and had to sit down again. After sitting there, my neighbor Jackie came out of her apartment and saw me sitting there with my head down between my legs and ran to assist me. "Seneca, girl … what's wrong?" she said out of breath from running down the hall way to get to me. In great distressed, I looked up at her and said, "I don't know Jackie. I'm bleeding and having abnormal stomach pains." Jackie was a big woman, not fat just tall as hell and she possessed a lot of physical strength. "Do you have someone to take you to the doctor?" Trying to stand up on the stairs I replied, "No girl, … I'ma pregnant. I am hurting and bleeding." as I bursted out in tears. "You're bleeding… you got to get to that hospital!" Jackie said picking up my purse and keys off the stairs. Holding my stomach I said, "Yeah I know, I will." as I held onto the rail with my other hand. Jackie looked down at her watch on her cell phone then looked down the hall to see if anyone was coming to help. "Seneca, I'm taking you to the hospital just give me a second to get my purse and check on my son then I will be ready." She sighed as she rushed off. I sat there on the second floor stairway bleeding, sweating and in lots of pain.
After about 30 second Jackie came running back to assist me. "Ok, I'm back, let's go baby?" she said. Holding back tears I nodded my head and then she helped me down to her car and put me into the backseat. In pain, I mustered up the words, "I… I gotta call D-Derron."

"Honey, let's get you to the hospital and you can call him later from there," Jackie said. Once we arrived at Northside hospital the nurse at the front station asked me what my emergency was. "I- I am," but before I could finish my sentence Jackie butted in and said to the nurse, "Look honey, she is pregnant, bleeding and in pain. She needs to see a doctor right now!" The nurse looked at her with a ill-mannered expression. "Miss… I need to talk to the patient." Jackie just glared at her and held her peace because she saw the nurse was short tempered and besides she was there for me. After the nurse took my temperature and blood pressure, she then said, "Okay, Ms. Martin, please come on back." Jackie helped me back room. The nurse yelled out to the emergency room nurses station, "I'm taking her back to room 134." The other nurses smiled and nodded and then continued doing paperwork. Once we were in the room I called Derron to let him know about my emergency. Jackie dialed the number for my on the hospital phone and hand the phone to me. When he answered the phone there was a lot of noise in the background. "Yes" he answered in a hurry tone. I cleared my voice and said, "Derron baby, I'm at Northside Hospital because I'm having stomach pains and bleeding." Before I could continue, he interrupted me and said, "Don't call me with that bullshit! I don't want to have anything to do with the situation until you have an abortion done." Jackie heard the whole conversation because the phone was up loud and just shook her head. Once he hung up the phone I began to cry because not only wanted him there, but needed him to be there. "That's a damn shame!" Jackie groaned. "What's the hell wrong with that nigga?" Blowing my nose I tried to answer her through the crying, slobbing and sniffing, but she couldn't understand me. "Fuck it Seneca! Give me the number and I'll call him!" After several attempts to call from the hospital phone, Derron refused to answer or when he did answer the phone he just hung right up. "Maybe I caused this on myself," I muttered to Jackie. She looked at me in astonishment and cried, "Baby girl..Nooo! You didn't cause his ass to bail out on you like this." Shaking my head I looked up at her at said, "Jackie, I did talk back at him a couple of week ago, and then I asked him if..." then I stopped and caught myself.

Jackie stood up and came near the bed and said slowly "You asked him what? Tell me, tell me Seneca! Look I'm here for you… can't you see that?"

"Of course, I can Jackie and I really appreciate you. It's just that my man… Well last week we had an argument and I asked Derron if he was gay or bisexual. I believe that had I not confronted him like that he wouldn't be acting like this. That's why I feel I bought this on myself." Jackie pulled up a chair to the bed and sat down quietly for a while, then she held my hand. She gave me the most confusing smirks and said,"Do you really think that he is? I mean… how do you know? Did you catch him with a man?" I answered, "No, but…" then by that time the doctor had knocked on the door and was coming in the room. "Hello Ms. Martin, how are you today? I'm Dr. Mathis and I will be examining you this evening."

I just laid there nodding my head every time the doctor said asked me something. I was bitter and confused and didn't know if I wanted to let the doctor try to save the baby or what. That's why I act like it didn't matter at first. "Now where does your stomach hurt?" Dr. Mathis asked. I pointed to the lower part of my stomach. "Are you pregnant honey?" She asked writing on my chart. "Yes I am… but I don't know how many weeks or months though" I said clearing my throat. She then asked Jackie to step out of the room while she examine me. While she examine me she told me that the bleeding had stopped and that it was probably just implantation bleeding. Dr. Mathis looked at my chart and said "Ms. Martin, I'm going to put in an order for you to go to ultrasound, so I'll be back shortly." I smiled and nodded my head, then she walked out of the room. Jackie came by the into the room and came over to the bed, "What did she say?" she asked then just when I opened my mouth to tell her, she cut me off and said with questioning tone, "Now girl, you gotta tell me about this gay shit!". "I don't really want to talk about it right now, but I will tell you later… k?" I said turning away from her. Jackie said that she going home for a while to check on her son for a while and that she come back to pick you when I was done. Just call me … okay?"

I answered okay, and then she walked out of the room. Once I was alone, reality kicked in so hard about Derron's feeling that I cried copiously; yet I still knew I had to pull myself together. So I wiped my tears with the hospital bed sheets and prepared myself to have the ultrasound. I guess deep down inside, a little part of me wanted to keep the baby. I tried calling Derron's phone several times. Sometimes he would pick up and I would here the football game playing on the TV and lots of people screaming in the background. After many unsuccessful attempts to contact him, I gave up. As soon as I pressed the end button on my cellphone, the ultrasound technician came into the room. "Helloooo… Ms. Martin, I'm Shemar and I will be taking you down to get your ultrasound done."

I grabbed my purse and the technician to roll me out of the room on the bed, down the hall to the ultrasound room. I was excited and sad at the same time. A part of me was hoping that it was a boy; but then at the same time, I didn't give a damn because I felt hopeless, alone and not cared about by Derron and at that time, nothing else mattered. Once I reached the ultrasound room the nurse instructed me to get on a table. She pulled up my hospital gown and put some cold wet gel on a little knob-like object. It was connected to a TV monitor where she and I could see the baby, or at that stage the embryo. My heart raced with excitement and my eyes were glued to the monitor. The nurse put the cold, gelled, knob on my small stomach and began moving it around while looking at the monitor. She asked, "Mrs. Martin, just out of curiousity, do twins run in your family?" I looked up nonchalantly and answered, "No. Why do you ask?" and she replied "Well, I asked because it look at though you are pregnant with twins." Trying to sit up on the bed quickly I shouted "What! Are… are you serious?!" She nodded yes and continued moving the knob around on my stomach. When I tried to get closer to the monitor and my wig got caught on a hook on the bed and almost came off. I was freaking out about this twin news and really didn't care. The nurse told me I was about nine weeks pregnant and that my twins were in two different sacs which probaly meant that they would be fraternal, but not necessarily. "Oh my God! How did this happen? What I'm I going to do with … five kids?! How did this happen?!" The nurse assured me that I would be fine and took me back to my room. I began to cry and thought about what I was going to do. I really wasn't sure about having an abortion, even so now because I was pregnant with two babies, but at the same time I didn't know how the hell I was going to take care of five children. Having a set of twins was a beautiful thing and I felt that they were God's blessing. I kept going back and forth with what decision to make as the ultrasound tech took me back to my room from ultrasound. A little voice in my head kept telling me that Derron was really going have a fucking fit.

I waited in Room 134 for about fifteen minutes before the doctor came back in. She pulled up the rolling stool and looked at my chart again. "Okay, Ms. Martin… it looks like you're pregnant with twins," she exclaimed with a smile. I tried to fake a smile back but I believed she saw right through it. "What's wrong, honey?" she said in concerned. "Oh nothing, just a little surprised, confused and apprehensive all at the same time" I said looking up at the ceiling as one tear rolled down my face. "Well, if I had to guess I would say that this was unexpected, right? Also, if I had to guess I would say that the father doesn't know or doesn't want any kids ... Am I right?" I looked directly into her green eyes and nodded twice and then I burst out in tears. The doctor held my hand and told me that she had confidence that I would make the right decision for me and the babies. As she got up from the stool, she walked toward the door and turned to me and said with a angelic smile and said, "Ms. Martin it could be worse. I'm a mother of three set of twins. You're going to do just fine."s then walked she out of the room. I lay there with my mouth open and my hands on my forehead. "Wow, I don't see how she does it. Shidd… couldn't be me! But what I'm I talking about… it is me."   The nurse had left a copy of the baby's ultrasound picture on the table within my reach. I got up to get dressed, then the nurse came into the room and released me 12 midnight.

I called Jackie to come pick me up. She answered, "Hey girl… you ready?" "Yeah, I'm ready," I said, in a low voice.

"Well okay, I'm on my way," she said, rushing off the phone. When she arrived at the hospital I was standing outside in front parking lot. She got out to open the door for me and said, "Hey sweetie, how are you feeling?, she said. "I'm okay… I guess." I answered. "By the way… what did the doctor say?" she inquired looking at me with seriously. Responding in a very uncomfortable way I said, "Well Jackie… they said that I was….. Oh, oh! but first…thank you so much for bring me to the doctor and if…" Jackie impatiently interrupted me, "Girl, stop beating aroung the bush… what did they say?!" "

I looked out of the car and said, "I'm two months pregnant and they gave me medicine for pain. I should be fine." "That's good child… you had me scared as hell," she said laughing out loud. She went on and on babbling about when she was pregnant and what she ate, how much she threw up, her baby's daddy, how she shaped the baby's head until I had to rudely interrupt her. "Jackie, Jackie," I yelled but she just kept on talking as if she had got caught up in hearing her own voice or something. "Yeah girl, the baby's head was so big and…" "

Jackie!!!" I screamed. "Girl, what the hell you screaming fo, I hear you, I'm sitting right next to you, damn!" she yelled back. "Sorry Jackie but I had more to tell you," I quickly said. She pulled over at a gas station. "What is it...you?" she said, looking at me wide eyed. "I'm pregnant with twins, and yes I do suspect Derron of being gay, or bisexual, but I have no substantial evidence other than me fingering him in his ass," I panicked. She looked at me smiling and said, "Wow ... twins. I always wanted twins. That's a beautiful thing Seneca, and you just got to keep them, but get rid of the pussy ass faggy! "

I laughed and began repeating, "I don't know! I don't' know! I don't know what to do with five kids, and Derron may not want them. In fact I know he don't want them or me. Jackie, he's going to leave me if I keep them. He told me this and I ... I don't want him to leave me. Besides ... I 'm in love him." Jackie was speechless; this time and didn't have much to say to me after that. Once we arrived at our apartment complex, Jackie parked the car, then turned to me and said, "Look, I can't tell you what to do with your life, but if I was you I would keep my babies and ditch that son of a bitch! You are stupid if you stay with him after how he showed you that he didn't give a fuck about you at the hospital." She then hugged me and I went upstairs to my apartment. After I entered my apartment I went to take a hot bath. I was so depressed and happy all at the same time. I truly wanted to keep the twins, but felt that I wouldn't have any support. For about three weeks afterwards, I went through depression, uncertainty, anxiety and crying about any and everything. I finally told everyone that I was pregnant with twins and they were almost all excited and happy for me. A few others shook their heads in shame. I needed support, but it seemed as if I didn't have any. While Belinda cried, "Have an abortion," Vanessa told me to keep the baby. I told my mother about the twins and she said that she was not keeping my babies if I had them. Not because she was mad at me; it's just that she was old and had always kept her grandchildren and now she was just tired of children.

The next day I called Derron. "Hello," he answered sounding irriated. "Uh... hey baby. I ...I got something to tell you." I was whispered scared to talk to him. "What is it, and hurry up; I got to go." he yelled in a snappy voice. "Well, I went to the emergency room and ... " He interrupted, "Man, go head on with that bullshit! I don't want to hear about no damn baby or you either!" "Derron, Derron, please listen for a second!" I yelled, holding back tears and trying not to cry. Derron gave a loud sigh, "Hurry up man… hurry up."

quickly muttered, "Baby… I'm pregnant with- with twins." A quietness came across the phone for about thirty seconds. Derron then said, "I'll call you back," and he hung up the phone. I never got a return phone call that evening. In all truth, I believed he was touched by the news, and I also believed that he couldn't deal with the fact that he was making me kill his twins but the evil in him was much stronger than the good.

As time went by Derron stayed at a distance from me. I grew more and more depressed by the day. One day I would be embracing the pregnancy and the next day I would be debating with myself about having an abortion. I didn't believe anyone could feel my pain or the torment I was going through on a daily basis. Up until the tenth week, I didn't go see the doctor or get any prenatal care. I was unsure about the decision I was going to make. I lay in my bed day after day just staring at the walls, while my oldest daughter cared for my little ones. Something about this pregnancy was different, though. I craved crab legs morning, noon and night and wouldn't eat anything else. Sad to say, my room was filled with the smell of crab legs, which was intensely excruciating for those who came in. I began falling into a deeper depression and was crying out for help. I barely got up to go to work, and when I did go my Captain wouldn't notice that I was sick and grant me time to get better by allowing me to just sit at my desk and file citations. I even remember being so sick that I wore wearing some shoes to work that were three sizes too big for me; I didn't realize it I had them on until my Captain noticed them. I was that sick, and I relentlessly slipped deeper into depression each day. Every day when I left work, I would go home and climb in bed to eat crab legs and wallow in a puddle of hurt, bitterness, anger, confusion and loneliness. I knew I was bad off when I started getting suicidal thoughts, and thinking to myself, that I might as well be dead, if I had to lose my twins and Derron too. I began plotting ways to plan my own death. This went on for approximately five days. I went through my files to find my insurance papers. I called the insurance company to check on my insurance plan. At this time, I was really considering sucide and just wanted to make sure my kids would be taken care of. I set my oldest daughter down and after carefully reviewing all the information in the policy, I told her that the insurance money with be split up in three ways between her and my other two girls. Of course, I didn't let them know what was going on with me.

One evening while coming home from work, I had an anxiety attack. I raced home just to lie down, but the twins were. I was three months pregnant, and my small frame was carrying around so much weight that I could barely climb the stairs up to my apartment. I looked like I was six months pregnant. I could hardly breathe and there was no one around to help at the time. I finally made it up the stairs to my apartment, and then I began to cry like I never cried before. Flashing through my mind were all the good and bad times I had with Derron my and images of the twins and what they would look like. "I can't go through this," I said, now lying on the bedroom floor in a fetal position. I decided to pick up the phone to call someone, anyone, for help; but ironically enough, no one would answered. I then got up off the floor, dried my face and went to take a bath. For days I stayed in bed, staring at the ceiling and wishing that I would die right where I was. My two youngest girls did not know what was going on with me. My youngest daughter, August who was only five at the time would lay by my side day and night cleaning up after me, singing to me and helping me to the bathroom and back to bed. She sometimes would fix me peanut butter and jelly sandwiches. This little girl somehow gave me hope to live, and strength to get up the each morning. I wanted someone, anyone to call, but strangely, no one did. I felt so alone and I even called my church for help to talk to the prayer line and to my surprise I got no results. No one from the church that Derron and I attended returned my calls either. I grew weaker in my body, emotions and faith. I just needed somebody to lean on and I felt that I needed just the 1 percent of support and a reason to want to live. Mainly, I really wanted to keep the twins, but didn't want to lose Derron.

I truly believed that God had ochestrated my situation as a set up for me. Because he didn't allow anyone to call or anyone to answer my phone calls when I cried out to them. I believe my daughter, August was a little angel God gave me to comfort me during this time, but I couldn't see that. I also felt that he wanted me to call out to him for help. I wanted to talk to someone just to vent to them but that was not God's plan for me and he had another one. One day my sister Veronica who I call, Ronni for short called to check on me. "What's up girl?" she said happy to hear from me. "Oh... hey. Nothing girl... just going through," I replied, trying to disguise my voice from crying. But after she heard my voice she knew something was wrong. Without hesitation she said "Look Sen ... Mama told me you was pregnant and that you're thinking about aborting it. But before you do please just get in the closet and cry out to God and he will help you!" We then talked about Derron and the baby. So that evening while everyone was away, I did exactly what she suggested. I went into my closet and begin crying out to God like there was no tomorrow, "God, please help me, I have nothing left. I need you God, please take away this pain from me. Please God ... please!" I cried tears streaming down my face and overflowing on the shoes on the floor of the closet in which I was in praying. It was the strangest thing I ever felt but as real as the morning sun to me. God dried my tears, and a peace came over me and assured me that I would be okay. I knew that God had heard my prayer that night. I started feeling the burdens of depression, anxiety, and suicide lift away from my mind, spirit and body. Shortly after getting out of the closet a voice came to me saying, "I thought you were going to have an abortion? Derron does not want you. You are going to be alone... like you are now." The thought of hearing that of hearing that overwhelmed me and I begin crying again. "I don't know what to do!" I shouted. "God you got to help, you just got to. This is not ... not your will for me ... is it? I can't take care of five children!" It felt as if Satan was trying to steal the peace that God had just given me. I sat up in my bed screaming at the top of my lungs. I didn't want to have an abortion, yet a part of me felt I had to. I said several time that I would go through with the abortion but I didn't mean it.

As time grew closer to the twelve week of pregnancy and I knew I had to make a decision because after 12 week I could have an abortion. Derron and I argued almost every day except when he would take the phone off the hook. The following week his family came to town and he didn't want to be bothered at all. The more I tried to call, the more frustrated I got. Derron acted more brutal than ever, and even when he did talk to me briefly he was more impertinent. I stayed away from him, but my belly continued to grow. Everywhere I went people looked at me with admiration because they were excited that I was having twins.

After everything had settled down some and his family left Derron and I discussed the abortion again. "I'm going back home for a while to deal with my family. I will go ahead and put up half of the money for the abortion, just make sure you get it done!" he demanded. We agreed that he would give me $250 for the procedure. The time was getting near for me to have the abortion and I was about 11 and 1/2 weeks into the pregnancy when we agreed that I would come to his house to pick up the money.

When I arrived at his house his oldest son, Jamal was there. He opened the door to let me in and when I went into Derron's bedroom, I saw him sitting on the floor counting money. "Ninety eight, Ninety nine… one hunderd," he counted out loud. He continued to count out another hundred and fifty dollars all in one dollar bills. He worked for a vending machine company putting snacks in libraries, car dealerships and stores. When he looked up at me and noticed the beautiful multi-colored, spaghetti-strap summer shirt I was wearing and then he said with a serious look on his face, "So… is this to be your maternity outfit?" I smirked and said, "No isn't I can't fit anything else." The outfit I was wearing was really cute and I was still sexy in it even if I was pregnant. Derron gave me the money and didn't even crack a smile. As I left the room, I layed the ultrasound picture of the baby twins on his dresser, and then I left.

The very next week Derron went to out of town, leaving me to deal with the consequences myself. The nigga didn't even have the heart to see me through the abortion. I wasn't allowed to go with him and it was his rules that I couldn't call him so much while he was away. He said he would call me when he felt he had a need to, or whenever he had time. I would follow his rules…sometimes.   The pressure was on at home. While he was away I did leave my bed for anything other than to use the restroom and to take a bath, sometimes. I stay in bed eating crab legs and drinking cokes. All I could think about was keeping the babies and I wanted him to be happy and accept them. After coming to the realization that he wasn't going to I started calling clinics to check the prices of the procedure and side effects.

I went back to work the next week and had a emotional breakdown, because I was going through so much at work dealing with a redneck racist Sargeant. My pregnancy wasn't helping the situation either. Trying to carry the weight of all of it was horrendous. The next day I called my girlfriend Debbie and I asked her to take me to the abortion clinic. That Saturday we went to the abortion clinic and the doctors examined me. The tall, white male doctor took an ultrasound of the twins, checked my blood and heart rate, and then told me to get dressed. After getting dressed, I sat on the table and he told me the appalling news. "Seneca, if you have an abortion you could hemmorhage to death, and I can't take the risk of that because I don't have enough doctors on staff in case something happens. Therefore, we will have to reschedule this until Tuesday of next week." I didn't know what to do at this point, I mean… I was afraid, and I was right at twelve weeks. I didn't want to disappoint Derron, either. I kept thinking to myself, "It's now or never, Sen." Time had actually run out on me and I had to either get it done that Tuesday with the understanding that I could hemmorhage to death or end up keeping the babies but losing Derron. I went home, thought about it and called him in Kentucky. Crying and sniffing, I decided to called and said, "Derron, I need to talk to you. I know you told me not to call you but baby I'm really scared. I went to the doctor and he told me that if I had an abortion that there's a chances I could hemmorhage to death."

I was thinking that after he heard this he would have a change of heart and tell me to keep the twins. Instead, Derron blew a gasket. He called me a bitch and a whore and accused me of trying to trap him. He also stated that if I had the twins he would decide whether or not to be in their lives and not to call him until they were born. I cried all night trying to decide what to do. I couldn't believe that the man I loved was actually telling me in so many words that he didn't give a fuck if I died he just wanted me to have an abortion! After hearing him say that, I just simply gave up altogether. I said to myself, well at least I don't have to kill myself because the doctors are going to do it for me and that way my kids will get my full benefits. I completed all the paperwork needed for my insurance and on the next Tuesday I headed back down to the abortion clinic with Debbie. She had strongly persuaded me that I needed to go through with it.

Once we arrived, I was in tears and the registering clerk asked for the co-pay of $250. I kept putting her off saying "Hold on, I'll be with you in a minute." The clerk grew impatient and walked off. While I was filling out the paperwork, I was talking to Debbie and crying because I knew that all odds were against me and no matter what I decided. Debbie put her arms around me and said, "Seneca, you are doing the right thing you don't need any more kids, girl." The clerk came back to the window and continued to pressure me to pay. I asked Debbie for the last time if I should do it. Again, she replied "Yes, it's the best decision for you." Uncertainly I gave the clerk the money and said a prayer in my head. When they called me to the back I turned around and looked at Debbie for I knew that it just might be the last time that I saw her face. I had come to accept that I was perhaps going to die but to me, it didn't matter any more. I was losing all the way around anyway and I was going to give up my life to please Derron, or I was going to keep my life and the twins lives yet lose their father.

While lying on the table with the big bright light over me I thought about what exactly the twins looked like and then I thought about God. "God please forgive me for this but I feel really forced to go through with it", I whispered.

The doctors stood on each side of the bed. "Hello Ms. Martin… I'm Dr. Bailey," and then he introduced the other doctor as Dr. Irvin. "I'm going to give you some medicine in your IV to put you to sleep and then we will proceed with the operation. At this time I couldn't talk because I had the oxygen mask over my face. I somehow mutter from underneath the mask and said, "Dr. Bailey … I think I need to I need to talk to…" but before I could finish my sentence I was knocked out like a light.

When the procedure was over I felt someone tapping me on the shoulder and calling my name. "Ms. Martin, Ms. Martin wake up honey it's over", a nurse repeated. I looked up at the nurse and around the room and saw other people lying in the beds. I didn't know if I had made it to heaven or hell or if I was still on earth. "Come on honey. Get up the procedure is over and I need you to sit up and drink this juice",said the nurse. The doctors that I had seen before I went to sleep were gone, and the room looked different. I glanced at the sheets that were covering me and   saw speckles of blood. I closed my eyes tightly and then I tried to sit up but a hideous pain came from my stomach. I could hardly move, but I opened my eyes in revelation. I had a unexpected thought, "Although I had given up on myself, God had not given up on me." I cried and stared down at the sheets. God saw me right through the procedure and held my hand the whole time. I'm sure he wasn't pleasd, but he knew my heart and heard my prayers as well. To this day I'm still in awe because of what God did for me. Even in my mess God still manifested himself before me and showed me grace and mercy. I had given up on living and was very shocked to that I had made it through the procedure. One hour later, I felt strong enough to get dressed and eat some crackers and lemonade. That's what they give you after an abortion to settle your stomach acid. Tons of sadness and despair flowed through my eyes and voice. I cried as if someone in my family had died but actually it was two innocent lives that had passed. Gasping for air, I had to try to get a hold of myself because it was over and there was nothing I could do about turning back the hands of time. Once I had calmed down I realized again for the second, third and fourth times that God had spared my life when I wasn't worthy of it. Obviously he still had a plan for me. I went out to the lobby and looked around for Debbie in the waiting area. "Seneca, hey I'm over here." Debbie yelled from the corner of the waiting room. I looked up at her and said, "It's done." She smiled and said, "You did the right thing."

After returning I came to the consious decision to let Derron go. He didn't give a damn if I lived or died and he certainly hadn't given a damn about the twins. I told my family to tell him that I was still in the hospital and that they hadn't heard anything from me. It was no longer his business. Also, I wanted him to feel guilty so for weeks I did not answer his calls because I wanted him to wonder whether or not I made it out of the recovery room and to live with the possibility that I had died. I continued this for about two months or so, going M.I.A. Derron would call and I would just stare at the caller I.D. and wouldn't answer. I was angry at him for pressuring me to give up our twins. However, I really could not face him to tell him how I felt. Derron must have called a twenty times a day. My anger at him was fueled by the thoughts of my twins, nightmares, and memories of the abortion room, the doctors, nurses and his selfishnes, yet I was too afraid to speak my mind because I felt that I would say something I might later regret. In truth, my anger stil wasn't enough to make me serious about leaving him though. I said it over and over, "I'm never seeing that no good motherfucker again." And then at night I would begin to miss him. I never called his phone yet I would replay the voicemail messages he left on my phone when he would try to contact me just hear his voice. I needed him to suffer the way he had made me suffer during my pregnancy and the abortion. To me, facing him was not an option because I wouldn't speak up to him unless he really pushed me. This was the right push but my heart was still soft for him. You would have thought that after everything I had being through with this nigga I would have dropped his ass quicker than dropping a past-due bill in a drawer that was full of other unpaid bills. At least that's what a woman who was fed the hell up would have done, but even after weeks of ignoring Derron I still somehow started missing him more and more.

One day I finally answered the phone when he called. Derron seemed not to be remorseful at all about the abortion; he was so nonchalant that I regretted even picking up the phone to answer and with his attitude you would have never thought that this was the same guy I'd met two years earlier. He acted as if he didn't give a damn about me, even though my behavior showed both him and I that I still was in love with him. In about one month I was fucking him again. You would have thought that after everything I had been through I would have had enough sense not to fuck with this man and he would have had enough sense to use condoms. He refused to use a condom and truth be told, it was so good that I really did not want it any other way. Besides, Derron was so in control of me that there was no way I was going to force him to wear a condom.

CHAPTER 15
THREE TIMES A FOOL

Around mid-January Derron and I were back on but he was more attentive as far as spending time with me. I believed that in a way he felt guilty about the abortion and was trying to somehow make up for it without admitting his wrong. Also, this time around he became more controlling than ever. I don't know if he thought that he was going to lose me or I was fed up. We started dating again, going back out to dinner and clubs, but he made it known that we were not just yet in a committed relationship. We were going to start off dating and he made it known to me that he was going to still see other females. He never expected me to have a problem with it, but just accept it and like his fool and sad to say, I did. He made it seem like that if I just played my cards right, one day we would be an exclusive couple again. Yeah, I was da-dupt, da-dupt as hell and knew I was dealing with a snake yet there was something about the way this snake kept sliding up and down in me that kept me being his prey. I made myself believe his lies, and I even believed the ones I told myself. Even though deep in my heart I had doubts but I loved him and wanted to make it work this time. He used to always say you have to do right to be on my team. I didn't want to be a part of his fucking squad, I wanted to be the whole team. The only one he needed and depended on. There were times when I would say to myself, "Fuck it!, I'm turning in my jersey and retiring my number, because I don't want to be on his fucking NFL team."

As time passed I made sure that I didn't do anything to jeporadize our relationhsip. Derron had full control over me, and I grew resentful towards him on the inside. I would always talk to myself when I was mad at him saying things like, Seneca, you are water while he is fire. I vowed earlier when I first met him that I would never argue with another man again and that if it came to me being wrong, wrong I would be. I wanted to please him because I felt that if I was pleasing him he would approve of and accept me for me. Derron had such a problem with me just being me. He always used to tell me that I was too white-girlish, or that I talked too proper, or that I was conceited. I could go on and on. I finally got to a point where I wasn't sure who I was supposed to be. Sometimes I would be at his house and he could be sitting on the sofa watching television. I would cater to him by getting beer, food, or giving him a massage on his back and his feet. At times I would be his personal nail spa and give his size fifteen feet a pedicure and out the blue Derron would say, "You are getting on my nerves." Of course, this would leave me confused as hell thinking what the hell did I do? I would ask Derron, "What did I do so wrong?". He would respond back by saying, "Nothing… you just being you, that's all." I would look at that negro in a statement of pissed O-F-F confusion and say to myself, "Who the hell I'm I supposed to be! I mean… if I can't be myself then who can I be?" I would just continue around about the house taking care of him and even though it hurt me, I wouldn't complain at all.

Derron did allow me to continue modeling and acting in some local things around Atlanta. I modeled for a while before while I was with Tony and stopped because Tony was so jealsous. Derron seemed at first to really support me in my modeling and acting gigs but he eventually grew very insecure just like Tony. Every movie premeire that I had to attend, Derron had to be right there with me and he even made us dress alike in the same colors everytime. At first I thought it was cute, but then my sister asked me about us dressing alike all the time and told me that people stopped doing shit like that in the 80's. After giving it some serious thought, I talked to him about and he said that when we went places, he wanted everyone in the world to know that we were together. I didn't contest it and mention it any longer, but went along with the flow.

I remember being on the set of a music video one evening. I was one of the principle models, therefore I just stood around and looked pretty while the artist sang to me or around me. I would bring or invite

Derron to come with me because he had this notion that he was going to lose me to one of the celebrity guys. "Child please, I'm more faithful than old yeller," I would murmur to myself. Derron made me give up modeling because it took time away from him. He always felt that whatever I was in, it would take me over and have all my attention. I was dedicated to whatever had my heart, including him. The sad part about this is that Derron knew this and still kept me on a tight leash; but when it came to him, the rules and leashes did not apply. I felt so resentful towards his ass, but did not want to be without him. He could go hang with his boys, and I better not act crazy about it or I better not ask to go either, unless he invited me to come along. I would call his phone and hear old hood-rats in the background all over him. He would just say, "Let me call you back," then hang up the phone. Another of his sayings was, "I don't play fair," and he really meant it. No matter how much I plead my case with him it was just not happening. Derron was so egotistical and cocky, you would have thought that this negro wore red and blue tights with an S on his chest under his white t-shirt and Macavelli jeans. But to be quite honest, I'm probably partly to blame for his behavior, because I treated him like royalty. I catered, kiss, sacrificed, and compromised my morals and beliefs to make him happy. It turned out that going back to him became a royal pain in my ass. My girlfriends always used to ask me why I bought this guy everything? Why did I cut and manicure his nasty ass, crusty, toenails and give him massages? Why do you put up with his shit for the most part, when he treats you like shit? I thought about it long and hard and the only thing that I could tell them is that when I love a man, I love hard and that I'm a very persistent chick anyway especially when challenged. But somehow I began to lose myself and eventually he became number one and I became number two and I loved him more than I loved myself which just made me a fool. Besides, this man was what I began to live for and I didn't want to lose him so I treated him better than I treated myself at times. I guess I sacrficed a lot for him, but at the times I felt he was the best things since crab legs and hot melted butter. My girlfriends use to say, "Girl, you ain't in love with that lizard, you're just love with that dick."

"Nope I loved him and I loved that dick," I would tell them. He would make sure he kept me addicted to his dick like crack. Every single time he went out and fucked up or made me mad, he would come over the following evening and dick me down. Although, I would be upset with him, his loving was really enough to pardon his behavior. It concerned me and I wanted him to stop, so I tried talking to him in a very loving matter about his problem, but he would just keep on drinking. Derron's drinking was getting the best of him and seem as if he wasn't in control of himself at times. It seemed as if the was trying to fill a void with the alcohol and there was really nothing I could have done about it other than what I had been doing. My father always told me that if a person is trying to control you that means his or her life is out of control and that person is searching for a balance; therefore they try to control you. He would hide his insecurities in such a barely discernible way that you would have never known that he was jealous and depressed all at the same time. "A person with holes in them can not be filled and you will drain yourself trying to pour into a person like that" my sister Phyllis would always say. Derron continued with his live life on the edge behavior and I grew more and more concerned, yet depressed while with him. He tried to play it off by being cool, cute and controlling, but I had him figured out before long. I knew he didn't have any game and that he was really unhappy with his life and his self. I was just in love with him that why I dealt with him. Everyone saw through his shit except for me. I was too over the hills and through the woods, but hadn't quite made it to grandma's house in love. My girls kept trying to tell me about the game he was playing, but I wasn't trying to hear that because he had me thinking that everyone, including my girls, wanted him and didn't want to see me with him. So at the time I did what any da-dupt, da-dupt or stupid in love female would have done. I believed my man and left behind the females that wanted him. I gave up my every desire, will and opinion about anything and everything. When he told me to drop them I would drop both my panties and female friends and that was the end of that. At least that's what I made him believe. I did not let him know what was going on, I just kinda played my role to deal with my female friends and then deal with him. Now, I played the dumb fox role but I was far from being dumb. I was just dickmatized to the point where Derron's name was written of over my pussy. Yet I still had my own mind, I just didn't express it to him. I just gave him the treatment that

I thought he liked and that he was used to having from me. Having been raised by a Muslim father who taught me that a woman should be submissive to her husband actually molded me into the woman that was able to be submissive to a man. Now on the other hand, my mama wasn't submissive at all . She fought my dad hard as hell any time he ever tried to make her submit to him. I guess I got of little of my mama in me too. I kept it tucked away, but trust me, I didn't take a lot of crap off of nobody except for Derron. I was committed to obeying his every rule and command.

CHAPTER 16
DISCERNING VISIONS

Derron was spending the majority of his time in the clubs, streets and with his friends and I was still trying to pursue my modeling career. One Wednesday afternoon I went to an audition in Buckhead to become a promotional model for Seagram's Gin. I had to hurry up and audition because I was meeting Derron at his house at 7:30 pm. After auditioning for the part one of the directors asked some of the other models and I to hang around the studio because he wanted to talk to us. Once we spoke to the director, he told us that we had been selected for the modeling gig. The director said that we would be leaving on the weekend and told us what we needed to have. "Leaving? I thought the shoot was going to be here in Atlanta," I mentioned to one of the models. "Naw, girl it's going to be in South Caroline on Myrtle Beach and I can't wait!", she exclaimed with excitement. I'm going home to pack now!" she yelled. I smiled at her and head to my car in the parking lot. I noticed that I had lost track of time and that it was 6:35 pm. After seeing the time, I just knew that I was going to be running late and needed to call Derron. "How the hell am I going to pull this off?" I said out loud walking out of the door. One of the female directors was standing outside of the door and heard me murmuring. "Are you alright?, she asked while looking down at a clipboard with all the models names and pictures on it. "You are Seneca, Right?" I smile and said, "Yes maam... that's right." She then when on to say that she over heard what I had said and asked me if I was going to be able to go n the shoot? I did not want her to have second though about me so I said, "Oh yes! Definitely I will be going. I didn't think it was going to happen this soon, but everything is cool. I just got to take care of some loose ends. That's all."

She looked at me with uncertainty in her eyes and said, "Okay… get it together sweetie. We will be leaving on Friday evening." I nodded my head and smiled and then I ran out the door as fast I could to my car. My cellphone began ringing so I looked at the caller ID and it was Derron calling. I didn't answer the first time he called because I was trying to figure out what to tell him. When he called back the second time I answered. "Hey Daddi, I was just getting ready to call you and-" I said. Derron interrupted me and said, "Mannn, I don't want to hear that shit! What took you so long to answer the god-damn phone? What the fuck are you doing?"

"I-I had my phone on charge in the car, Daddi. I'm on my way baby, I took my mom to the grocery store," I said, in a timid voice. "Well, I'm going over Kenar's house. It's almost 7:00 and your ass ain't here?" Derron said. "But baby…" I began trying to plead. "Don't baby me! You should have had your ass here already. I got to go. I'll talk to you tomorrow," he said and hung up the phone. I sat in my car with tears in my eyes, I became upset and said, "Well fuck it! That nigga is acting like that then I might as well go to Myrtle Beach." Then I went home to pack.

The next day I didn't hear from him so I texted him and told him that I was going to be with my father on Friday and Saturday. He texted me back, ok and I went shopping afterward to get some things that I might need on the trip. I kept thinking that Derron is going to shit a brick if he knew I was leaving town. Truly, I did not know what to do and although I had made up my mind to go the night before I still wrestled with the fact that Derron wouldn't allow me to go if I went to him with the truth.

When Friday came I took off work to do some last-minute babysitting arrangements for my kids like making sure someone was going to care for them while I was away and that they had everything they needed. It was around 4 o'clock in the afternoon, I texted Derron again. This time I texted I love you Daddi, but he didn't text me back. I blew it off by saying well he's probably in a library somewhere filling the vending machines and can't text me back.

At the last minute, I remembered that I needed a pre-paid phone to take with me because my Metrocel PCS phone really didn't give me the permission to speak as freely in another state and I needed to contact my babysitter and family just in case of an emergency. Also, I was going to try to eventually try calling Derron again. After purchasing the phone, it was time for me to go and meet up with the directors and models at the studio. Since I already had all my bags packed, I headed down I-20 west to the meeting spot. As soon I arrived at the studio I received a text from Derron. My eyes lit up so bright and I smiled because I knew he was responding to my text from earlier. I opened the message on my phone opening to read those three words that I had sent to him earlier, instead the message read, ok. I blew it off because Derron didn't express feelings like that for his own reasons. He was a guy who would show you some love before he told you anything. I accepted and dealt with it, but I still wanted to hear it from time to time.

I parked my car and then I got out to put my bags on the charter bus that we were traveling in. It was time for us to leave so everyone got on the bus and began talking and finding seats to sit in. I took a seat near to back of the bus because I was kind of sad that I had lied to Derron and felt it was a shame that I hide something that was a part of me and made me happy. Also, as the bus started pulling off I began to miss him, but there was no turning back now. I was heading to Myrtle Beach without his knowledge and without his blessings. Everyone on the bus was excited about the trip and the modeling gig. They all were laughing and talking about the trip and the shoot; I listened in and at times I would laugh out with them just to hide my sadness and frustration with Derron. After about 6 hours of traveling, every one began drifting off to sleep. Then we were woken up by the director's voice yelling for everyone to wake up. I opened my eyes and looked at the time on my cell phone. I called my voicemail from my pre-paid phone to check to see if Derron had called. "You have two messages in your mail box," the voicemail operator said. I was anxious to hear them because I thought just maybe one of them, if not both messages was from him. The first message played, "Girl, this is Vanessa, give me a call." I frowned and deleted the message. Then the second messages began to play. "This next message just got to be from him," I hoped silently to myself. He hadn't physical spoken to me all day, so I just know he was wondering what I'm into. The message played, "Mommy, I just wanted to say goodnight and I love you." It was my little girl

Amondi calling to say goodnight. When I heard this I smiled but I was sad at the same time because I was really hoping that Derron would have left me a message by now.

We had arrived at the hotel, and everyone was getting their belongings off the bus. One of the models came to me and out of concern she said, "Seneca, you seemed worried about something and I 'm not sure what it is, but if you don't snap out of it you're not going to do well in your shoot. Trust me, I know because I've been distracted before and fuck up on my shoot." She cried. As I listened my eyes began to get watery. I quickly wiped my eyes and thanked her. Once we all were assigned to our rooms, the director said, "Ladies, at noon tomorrow, please be ready for your shoot." We all said okay and went to our rooms to get some sleep. The next day I woke up at 10:30 a.m to get dressed. Some of the models were up and some were still asleep. My first thought was to call and check on my little girls and to call Derron. When I finished talking to my kids, I called his home phone and I got no answer, then I try his cellphone and he did not answer it either. I left a message telling him to give me a call but I didn't leave my pre-paid cell number. I didn't want to get questioned about the number, so I told him to call my regular cell number.

Around noon we were all on the set of Myrtle Beach doing our shoots. I had such a great time and my pictures were absolutely gorgeous and for a moment I forgot how sad I was about Derron and enjoyed myself. The shoot lasted for about four hours and everyone was tired but they all kept giving the directors and photographers the best of themselves.

"Okay, this is the last take and then we are going to wrap it up," shouted the director. I was happy and felt very successful about the shoot. When it was over, we all relaxed on the beach and then we went to eat at The Miranda Towel, a restaurant that was right on the shore of the beach. We were going to be heading back to Atlanta last that afternoon. After eating we all went back to the hotel to pack it up, so I called Belinda to see what she was doing and to tell her about the shoot. She asked me if I wanted to go out that night when I got back in town. I told her that I would let her know by 8 p.m because I really wanted to get up with Derron. She said okay and then we hung up. I called Derron's cellphone once again and this time he answered. "Hey

Daddi, what are you doing?" I asked. "Chilling, what's up?" he said as he seemed to have been smoking a blunt. "Nothing Daddi, I just wanted to touch base with you that's all and wanted to see you this evening. Is that cool?" I said talking low and at full speed because I didn't want him to hear the girls in the background. He replied, "Uhh... I'll let you know." By then the director was coming into the room and was getting ready to make an announcement. I didn't want him to hear her so I told Derron that I would call him later and quickly hung up the phone. "Ladies, we will be leaving in 2 hours, so please make sure you have all your belongings," the director said then walked back out of the room. I took a shower and packed up my things, and then I decided to tap a power nap until it was time for us to leave. While I was asleep I had a dream about Derron. I dreamt that I was at his house and there were three fat black girls with blonde wigs standing in his living room with me. They were telling me that Derron was gay and at the same time I saw the silhouette of a tall man bringing Derron a plate of food. My friend Belinda was in the dream but I didn't know exactly where. One of the models shook me and told me that it was time for us to leave the hotel and headed back to Atlanta. As I was leaving out of the room I figured that I might as well go on and call Derron. He answered the phone saying, "Yeah, what's up?" with a lot of music in the background. "Hey Daddi, am I going to be with you tonight?" I asked. Slowly he replied, "Nope. My boys and I are heading out to the club." I became quiet on the phone and my heart was heavy because I really wanted to be with him, but at the same time I was pissed. Instead of doing my normal begging routine I asked him if it would be ok if if I went out with my friends.

"Mannnn... stay your ass home and read a book. Naw, you better not bring your ass out!" I continued holding the phone in silence and listening to him rant and rage because I couldn't say exactly what I wanted to say because I was on the bus. Derron all of sudden asked me if he allowed me to go out where was I going. I answered wavering, "I guess I'll go to the 20 Grand on Old National. Then I told him that one of my friends was having a birthday party there." Derron instantly began yelling, "That's my fucking club! You better not bring your ass up there! You hear me?" My voice cracked and I answered very slowly and said, "Yes Daddi, but ..."

Derron hung up the phone and I called Belinda back. "Hey girl, I can't go to the club with you," I said sniffing. "Why Seneca, what's wrong?" she asked. I didn't answer and just repeated to her that I couldn't go. "Derron said you couldn't go, uh… Didn't he?" She inquired again and I still did not answer but just held the phone. Belinda then just came out and said, "Seneca, I'm not trying to offend you, but you are stupid girl to let this man have you so fucked in the head. I'm your friend but you better stop letting him do you like. His fucking ass is doing whatever he wants to do!" then she told me that she had to go feed her kids and we hung up.

When the charter bus arrived in Atlanta it was around 11:00 pm Saturday night. I went to my car and loaded my bags in the trunk and headed home. It was so late that I decided to call the babysitter the next morning to pick up the kids. I tried calling Derron back but he didn't answer. I started thinking that Belinda was right and I am a damn fool to be stuck on stupid with Derron while he's living his life." I also came down on myself because I was supposed to be happy about getting this modeling gig and here I was the whole time thinking about his ass. The fact of the matter is that some other young lady didn't have that opportunity and here I was being ungrateful. They could have very well considered someone else, instead they choose me. I called Belinda back and told her that I had decided to go to the club. She started yelling and saying that she thought I would come to my Aries senses. We laughed about it and then I told her that I would call her as soon as I arrived.

CHAPTER 17
WHEN THE TABLES TURNED

I grabbed my bags and before leaving the director told me that my check will be mailed out next Tuesday. I then got into my car and drove home to dress. Derron didn't call me anymore that evening which made me more anxious to get up and out to hit the street. I quickly took a bath got dressed and went to pick up Belinda. Belinda and I arrived at 20 Grand a little after mid-night and the line to get in the club were extremely crowded. The music was loud and young people were every where. I was quite hesitant to go in and on my way inside the club I wrestled with thoughts of turning around and going home or confronting Derron head on just in case I ran into him. I knew Derron was going to be totally pissed about me being in the club. Especially since it was his so–called club but I was willing to face.

We finally made it inside the club and Belinda was already hyped up to go to the dance floor. "Seneca, I'll be right back. I'm going to the bar to get a drink. Do you want anything?," she said while trying to drop it like it was hot.

"Uh No… I'm good but thanks," I answered as she left me at the entrance of the club. I walked over to the left side of the club to get in a corner so I wouldn't be seem by him just in case he was walking around as he often did while clubbing. I was scared, but I felt a small sense of power because I had made a decision for myself regardless of what Derron had said. I saw Belinda walking back towards the entrance looking for me, so I swiftly walked up to her lead her to the corner where I stood waiting. "Girl… you crazy are as hell! Let me find a table," she said laughing and walking towards the tables. We found a table directly in front the dance floor. As I sat down I asked her to sit behind me so that she could block me from being seen. We both were people-watching and observing the panorama, when without warning Belinda nearly jostled me out of my seat. "Seneca, Seneca... there's Derron!" My heart nearly jumped out of my chest and ran out the front door. I slid down in my seat and murmured,"Where?" Belinda told me to turn halfway around and peek over her shoulder. I positioned myself to do so and when I looked over her shoulder I saw my dream being played out right in front of me. Derron was kissing, rubbing and hugging all over some extremely fat, black girl with blonde hair. Exactly how I had seen it in my dream earlier that evening when I went to sleep. While Belinda and I drove to the club, I had told her about the dream as well. Truthfully, I didn't know whether to laugh or to start crying because this girl was so fucked up from the toe up. I couldn't believe that this man that I had to stay up on pedestal for would downgrade to a lower model female just because it had a for sale tag on her. After all he upgraded in everything when he met me. I wasn't about to confront him because I knew better than that, but I want to just observe his behavior. Belinda looked at me with neurotic eyes and said, "Seneca, this is your damn dream!"

"Yes, yes... I know, I know," I said with tears forming in my eyes. "Quick, duck down! He's looking over here," she yelled. I ducked and then Belinda spurred that we needed to find me someone to dance with. I didn't want to do that because I didn't want to upset him or challenge him in that way because I knew in the end, I would lose or be placed on dick, don't call, or don't come over restrictions. "Look, if you don't do something, you're going to look real damn stupid," Belinda yelled at me. After quickly thinking about it I told her to pick someone that he would consider competition and someone with long braids just like him. I hid behind a menu that was on the table and continued to keep my eyes on Derron, while Belinda got up and looked around for the guy we could use. When she returned she brought back a guy whose body was well toned and he was good looking. But most importantly, he had shoulder length long designed braids in his hair. He was nicely dressed in a baby blue linen suit. When they walked up to the table, Belinda looked at me and winked her eye and then introduced me to the guy. She told him that I had noticed him from across the room and wanted to dance with him. He then introduced himself as "Q"; then we went to the dance floor. The Belinda came up on the dance floor with some other guy and we danced with our backs to each other because she was watching Derron and trying to let me know when he actually noticed me. After about ten minutes of dancing, Belinda informed me that Derron had noticed me on the dance floor and that he was watching. Although it was childish, I felt good about turning the tables on him. While dancing with Q I started visualizing a scene from this movie called, *Two Can Play that Game*. There was a scene where Vivica Fox and her friends were at a party and her ex-boyfriend walked in with his friend. Her ex was dancing with a girl while she and her friends looked on. After he finished dancing, Vivica and him talked briefly. She began to walk off and then intentionally dropped her purse and out fell a condom. It caught her ex off guard and totally brain fucked him. He was now not enjoying his evening and was concentrating on who the luck guy would be at the party to end up sleeping with her. This tactic fucked up his whole evening thereafter. Now I was doing something a little bit different, but just as effective. I made sure Derron was watching me, and then I rubbed my hands all through this guy's braids, and danced very sexy with him. I grabbed him by the hand and led him to the other side of the club. This move is called, "Fuck Him Up" according to the movie, Q and I talked in a dark corner on the other side of the club. I decided to do a count down move t make Derron to come running up behind me. After about a minute had passed, I started counting down in my head while talking to this new guy in the dark, discreet corner. Ten, nine, eight seven, six, five and just before I got to four I heard a deep male voice call my name. I turned around and Derron was standing right behind me. "Uh…Hey Seneca" he said with a shake voice and shocked look on his face. I smile and said, "Hi," and thinking silently that this shit really does work. He responded in a warranted way and then he walked off. Our plan had paid off and he had done exactly what I wanted him to do; which was to respond to me. Neither, Derron or I could have ever imagined me defying him to this level, but I was tired of the bullshit with him especially when I was doing all the things I was supposed to try to please him emotionally, physically, and mentally. Derron was out of sight I told Q that I wanted to go back on the other side to sit down at the table. When we arrived back at the table, Q wanted to go something to drink, so he walked up to the bar and as soon as he left Derron rushed and sat in his seat and started cussing me out. "Didn't I tell you not to come to my fucking club? What the hell you doing rubbing your hands all through that nigga's braids? You done fucked up bitch!" Derron screamed in rage. I didn't say anything. In fact, I couldn't say anything because the music was deafening and he was talking so fast that I was scared he was going to beat my ass. Oh shit I think I've gone too far, I thought to myself. I then started saying fuck it and fuck him… It is what it is. Derron saw that Q was coming back towards the table and he quickly got up and left. When Q got to table he noticed the devastated look on my face and asked me what was wrong. I told him the whole deal with Derron, the dream and how we chose him to dance with. He shook his head and laughed and then told me that he knew we were using him to make someone jealous. I dropped my head and told him that he was absolutely right and apologized. "No need to apologize, it was my pleasure," he said. While he was talking I was looking around the club to see if I could spot Derron but there were no signs of him. Maybe he's in a corner watching me from afar, I thought. I was very uncomfortable just sitting there talking to this guy. Belinda finally came back to the table. "Heyy… what happened!" she asked dancing to the music. "Did he fall for it?" she continued. Not feeling good about what I had done, I answered her with heaviness in my chest. "Yes, it worked like a charm." Q and Belinda burst out laughing. It was going on 3 am in the morning and we all started walking around the club. I spotted Derron in the pool room playing pool with his friend Kenar, and some other people. We walked into the pool room and as I walked closer to them I noticed that Derron was talking to some hood-rat girl wearing a broke down wig. I smirked and said to myself that he is trying to find some competition for me but I didn't get upset at all. I walked over toward him and told him that I needed to talk to him." He grabbed the girl's hand and told me that his friends didn't want to hear that shit and then they walked off. Belinda yelled out to him, "Heeyyy… Derron" but he ignored her and kept walking. I guess she was trying to make the girl say something to her because Belinda didn't mind a fight at all. After they left my mind was now going against me and I was feeling really terrible about the game

I played and I wished that I had never done it. We decided to leave the club and go home. Q walked us to my car and then he and I exchanged numbers. He was down in Atlanta for his birthday and he was heading back to North Carolina the next day.

CHAPTER 18
LET THE GAMES BEGIN

Derron and I didn't speak for about two weeks after the club scene. I've never been the type to hold grudges or anger for a long period of time. I guess it just wasn't what I'm made of. The night of the club incident I had the strength to say it was over between him and I but after days had passed with no contact I began to weaken for him. I tried calling and calling but he didn't answer. I started texting him but he wouldn't text me back. In the meantime, I started talking to Q on the phone. He was also in a relationship, but he and I became phone buddies. We talked about my situation with my man more than anything. He seemed to have taken interest in what I was going through with Derron and offered his advice and techniques to try to get through to him. Q was a loving guy who really cared about his relationship with his girlfriend as well as with others too. We would exchange information, advice, and supported each other emotionally. I believed this was because Q was born under the sign of Aries, just as I was. We had so much in common as far as being really giving and altruistic in our relationships. In the beginning, he wanted to take our friendship further and so did I, but I was too wrapped up in Derron to give anyone else a fair shake.

One evening around 8:00 pm I was while talking to Q at the shop that he barbered at and he advised me to go over to Derron's house and talk to him. He said that if I needed him to that he would let Derron know that he was only a friend. I took his advice and headed over to Derron's house around 9:00 pm. I pulled into his subdivision and I saw his car, but I also saw another car right next to his in his driveway. My fucking heart began racing. I knew he had company and I didn't want to just go knock on the door, but I had no choice due to the fact that he wouldn't answer the phone. I parked my car, and then I walked up to door and rang the doorbell. After about thirty seconds Derron open the door and stuck his head out. "What do you want? I got company," he said in a malevolent way. When I heard this, my heart dropped into my stomach because my fear before walking to the door was true. After I gathered my mental stablity I said in a soft voice, "We need to talk." He repeated that he had got company, but this time he said it in a deeper and louder voice. I held my head down trying to think of the next thing I could say to get through to him. When from behind the door I hear a female voice saying,"Baby, let her come in." My heart dropped another fifty feet; only this time it was in my knees. My legs began shaking like a leave and my voice wavered when I asked, trying to sound calm, who was that?" He replied telling me that it was none of my goddamn business, and then he told me to go on and play all the niggas' hair again! I tried several times to interrupt him, but he kept telling me that he didn't have anything to say to me. He shut the door in my face and I walked away with a single tear flowing down my face. Damn it seemed like he's turned the tables back on me, I gathered in my thoughts as I got into the car. I won the battle, but I'm losing the war, I yelled out loud. Within seconds, Derron had made me feel bad as hell and I now felt like I had done something wrong when the only thing I was doing was finally standing up to him and giving him a taste of his own medicine.

Several weeks passed by and I had not heard from Derron. My phone buddy Q continued talking to me and on the phone. Offering me as much advice to get me through the day and sometimes, the week.

One Sunday morning while I was still sleep in bed someone rang my doorbell. I didn't have company over like that, and surely I wasn't expecting anyone. As I went to the door I asked very hesitant, "Who is it?" Then in a very low voice I heard someone tell me to open the door. My eyes got wide and I stuttered as I said, "Ho-hold on." It was Derron at the door and as if was getting ready to open the door I remember that I had not brushed my teeth or washed my face, so I then rushed into the bathroom to take care of my hyigenes. When I opened the door he walked in slowly looking around to see if anyone else was there. "What up?" he said still speaking in a low voice. "Hi Daddi," I said and then I hugged him around his waist. He made his way back to the bedroom and started taking off his size 15 Nike shoes and his red hooded sweatshirt and jeans. I was so happy to have him there that I forgot to be mad with him. He positioned himself on his back while lying on my bed and was strangely quiet. I began rubbing his dick through his boxers when he told me take off my panties. He then got up and put his head directly between my legs and begins sucking my pussy. I didn't know what to make of it so I went with the flow. He made awe-inspiring love to me for about two hours. Afterwards, we laid there holding each other and I wanted so bad to talk about the situation at hand, but I was to afraid. I was still trying to think of something to say to break the ice between us, so I asked him if I could ask him something. Yes he answered, but advised me that he didn't want to go into no heavy shit. I paused for a second to filter my questions and then I told him that it was cool. I sat up on the bed and began rubbing his braids and then asked him was that girl still at your house. I waited for his response. "Umm… Not really. Seneca that girl doesn't have any place to stay and she's helping with the bills; so I let her rent the room upstairs", he said looking uncomfortable. I was getting ready to ask him another question when he interrupted and said, "That's enough questions now," in a strong, I-mean-what-I-say tone. Inside I was dying to get unanswered questioned out, but I wanted to enjoy my time with him as well, so I let it go. After about four hours Derron left to go home. I felt sad in the end, but then agitation kicked in. However there was nothing I could do or say about it. After he left I thought about this female living over there with my man. I wasn't sure anymore but letting him go was not an option for me because this was the man that I loved. I continued seeing Derron throughout the year but not knowing where I stood with him and although I often ask he never would give me a straight answer. "Just play your cards right," he would say. He gave me a false sense of hope, but never assured me that we had a solid foundation as a couple and besides, this girl was still living in his townhouse and he claimed that he wasn't sleeping with her. Derron and I would go out to dinner, movies and even back to his church. I can remember going to dinner and making love in her car on Memorial Drive. That's why I kind of believed him about the relationship that he had with the girl.

Valentine's Day was coming up and Derron was my one and only prospect and had been for three years straight. I was anxious and really wanted to get him something special so I went to the mall and bought him a $1700 men's diamond ring. I was excited and hoping that we would go somewhere nice but he never showed up on Valentines Day. I was upset but I was learning how to be numb to my emotions. Two weeks later, he showed up with no explanation and empty-handed. I tried asking him why he didn't show up but he kept avoiding the question,I did'nt push it.I ended up giving him the ring because it bought for him and I wanted him to have it despite of the way he treated me. It seemed that every month that passed things got worse between us. He was often missing in action, wouldn't answer his phone, or call. In my heart in knew something was wrong, but I couldn't seem to just let it go that easy because I knew I was lovable, caring and that I took care of his needs. So I couldn't understand why he was treating me this way. I felt that something mentally had to be wrong with him, because I believed that when you loved someone you just didn't treat them bad and I showed this guy all the unconditional love that I every shown anyone. In fact I loved him more than I have loved any man. I even kept up that twisted sick finger fucking because it was now mandatory and he made me feel that I had to accept it or leave him. I choose to deal with it because I was in denial and so much wanted it not to be true.

I later learned that he was evicted from his apartment townhouse and that he would be moving in with his female friend named, Shanna. I didn't find out about the girl living there until a month or two later. Derron had people who felt that he wasn't treating me right and they just wanted to give me the heads up on what he was doing. He thought he was pulling the wool over my eyes but everyone knew he was treating me wrong. Girls that he knew told me where he lived and who he lived with. They also had proof of it all, so this wasn't a haters' move.

Derron and I were on and off throughout the whole year. I really wanted my relationship to work or maybe it was just the challenge of it all. Oftentimes I would call him and the girl would answer his. We would get into it on the phone about him but Derron would continue tell me that there was nothing between them. I knew better but again there was nothing that I could do about it. Derron gave me hope that it was going to be me and him if I played my cards right. That's why distinguishing whether he was gay or not was so damn hard because he carried himself like a thug. He was hard, tough, caring yet distant and his appearance was that of a thug. However, still wanted me to finger him in his ass and it like I was trapped doing something that I was so against and I was losing my identity to him.

CHAPTER 19
THE DEVIL'S ADVOCATE

Derron started letting me off of his tight leash around the end of April. I was allowed to hang out a more with my girlfriends out at clubs as long as it wasn't at his clubs. I also started back pursuing my modeling and acting gigs again since Derron was occupied with what he had going on at home. By May, I got offered a part in a stage play called, "Letting Love Happen." The show was coming up soon at the Rialto theatre and Derron wanted to come see me in the play, so one Tuesday after rehearsal, I got him free tickets that would have cost him $27 dollars at door to purchase. Derron came over that following Wednesday and we had dinner, talked and made love all that evening. It was just like it old times again and we were getting along and communicating better this time around. Even though I had reasons to doubt his truthfulness, there was only so much I could control and arguing with him would only run him into the arms of another woman.

The play was that Friday at 7:30 pm. I was excited because my baby was coming to see me perform. I asked my girlfriends if they wanted to come but they felt since Derron was going to be there, there was no need for them to come. I didn't go to work that day because I wanted t stay home prepare for my show. I called Derron throughout the day just to touch base with him and to make sure he was coming. He assured me that he would be there front and center watching me do my thing. Later that evening, I got ready to go to the Rialto for the dress rehearsal and run through some quick lines with my colleagues. After finishing practice, it was almost time for the show. I was so focused and nervous about the show that I didn't give any thought as to whether or not Derron was coming.

The show was soon to start and everyone was positioning themselves to perform at their very best because for this could one day could be an award-winning stage play. I heard the director say ok, we will be going on in 20 seconds. Everyone got in place and waited for the curtains to open. Lights, Camera and Action! We were on stage and hundreds of people filled the audience. I smiled harder than I ever had before because I was fulfilling my passion for acting and dancing and I just knew Derron was in the audience. The show was a hit and we received a standing ovation.

After the show was over people were coming backstage to congratulate their friends and family members. I had changed clothes and was waiting for Derron to come backstage at any minute. I stood there smiling and talking to other crew members about the show, but there was no signs of Derron. About twenty minutes had passed and my heart told me that Derron was not going to walk up those stairs. My friend Deena walked over to me and told me that I did a great job and then she said that everyone was going to Buckhead to celebrate. "Are you coming?"

"Uhh… wait one second," I told her and then I rushed to the dressing room to get my cellphone out of my purse to call Derron. I had several missed calls but I wasn't concerned with that because none of the calls were from him. I dialed his number over and over and got no answer. Deena walked into dressing room and I told her that I had to go home and get my kids because my babysitter needed to leave. I lied to her because I was upset about Derron and wanted to be available if and when he called. "Okay, I understand. We'll do something together next week," she said in a joyous tone. She hugged me and then I got my bags and walked out to my car. I wondered every second and minute about what had happened to Derron. I had unanswered questions and my heart was filled with anxiety and confusion, so I called his phone again. This time I left a message on the phone, "Baby, where are you? What happened I looked for you in the show and I didn't see you, please give me a call. I love you. Bye." I drove all the way home in tears and angry at the same time. I didn't know if he had done this on purpose or if something had really happened. When I arrived home it must have been 1 o'clock in the morning and I couldn't sleep because I was worried about Derron. I called a few more times before I finally fell asleep.

The next day I woke up with him on my mind and wondering about what could have happened and why he would do me like this. I tried calling him again around 12 noon and then at 6 p.m, then 9 p.m and again at 12 midnight. My whole day was messed up so I stayed in bed and took Tylenol PM to make me sleep until the next morning so I couldn't feel any pain. After trying to bury the memory of Derron's no call, no show from the Friday night, I woke up and it was Sunday morning. I decided to try to pick myself up before I became really sick and depressed. After struggling to get myself together I decided to go to church. My church service started at 11:00 a.m so I hurried out of bed and took a shower. I then prayed and asked God for direction and comfort before leaving out of the house. I must have driven about fifty miles an hour down I-285 with thoughts of Derron and his whereabouts drizzling through my head. I noticed the time on the clock as I looked down to search the radio station for Gospel music and it dawned on me that the church service would be over in the next thirty minutes or so. I hit the accelerator a little harder to try and make it there in time, but as I was approaching the Memorial Drive exit I suddenly thought about going to Victory Baptist church. That was the church where Derron and I attended service on several occasions and since I was really running late, and more than likely I wasn't going to make my church service on time so I decided to head to his church instead since it was closer. As I prepared to exit onto the Memorial Drive ramp, my anxieties set in and sweat from my hands moistened the steering wheel. The anticipation of seeing Derron made me nervous and I almost turned around but I didn't want to miss the service at any cost. I decided to call someone to get advice as to what I should do and called my cousin, Tonya. When I dialed her number and she answered,"What's up cuz?" I then laughed and said, "Oh nothing much. I'm on my way to church and, and…" but before I could finish what I was saying Tonya interrupted me by saying, "Oh good I'm on my way out the door now. I'll meet you there!" We attended the same church, but she lived right down the street from it. I responded quickly by saying, "Hold up T, I'm not going to our church. I'm going to go to

Victory Baptist. You know the church Derron and I go to sometimes."
This was one place that he didn't put restrictions on me. Silence came
over the phone for about a second or two. I said "T … Are you there?"
She answered with a very dry voice sarcastically, "Yeah I'm here, and
what the hell are you going there for?" I explained to her about the
heaviness that was on my heart, and my situation regarding the church
service. She then said she understood, and sarcastically said, "Alright
now, don't go up there wind-milling and thangs like that." We both
laughed as I was entering the church parking lot. I drove around the
lot to see if Derron's car was there, then I told my cousin that I didn't
see his vehicle, so it should be okay to go on in to the service. Once I
arrived inside the church lobby people were standing out in front of the
sanctuary and seemed to be waiting to go in. Shortly after walking in
I was greeted by an usher saying, "Good morning, please wait quietly
out here while they are having prayer in the sanctuary." She went on to
say that once the prayer was over everyone would be allowed to enter
the service. I nodded my head in agreement and told my cousin that I
would call her after the service.

Waiting in the front lobby of the church, I could see everyone
who walked in the church and just the thought of seeing Derron there
brought trepidation to my heart. I waited patiently to be seated by
the usher, but I was still nervous about being there and I somehow
managed to drop my cellphone on the floor as I stood in the lobby
area. I stoop down to pick it up and as I rose I looked towards the
entrance and almost fainted. Right before my eyes, in slow motion, I
saw Derron walking into the church and he wasn't alone! There was a
girl with him. One thing for sure; it wasn't me. He was wearing his 4x
white button down shirt and Machavelli jeans and his hair was braided
as usual to the back and this bitch was walking right beside him as if
she was his girl. My heart pounded with annoyance, rage and fear all
at the same time. "What the fuck is this?",I questioned myself. I didn't
want cause a scene, so I quickly walked around the corner so that he
wouldn't see me and I opened up my cellphone to call my cousin back.
I felt an uncontrollable flow of tears stream down my face. When Tonya
answered the phone, I told her in an unnerved voice that Derron had
just walked into the church with a girl and I didn't know what to do.
Talking under my breath I repeated over and over to her, "What should

I do, T? What should I do?" She said in a calm voice, "Girl, there is nothing wrong with you being there at church and besides, you were just with the nigga!" I told her that he may still be shocked to see me there, and caught up in anger since he was getting ready to be busted. I heard the usher telling a lady that the prayer was over and they were getting ready to let people enter the sanctuary, so I knew I had to act fast. I pulled myself together very quickly and told myself that I had just been with him on Wednesday, and I had no reason to hide or be afraid. I pranced around the corner and approached Derron. When he saw me his eyes literally popped out of his head. I smiled and said, "Hello Derron." He didn't respond, as if his tongue was glued to root of his mouth. He gestured for us to walk over near a corner to talk, so I followed him. The girl that he was with was talking to some other fat white rodent. I said to him, "Baby, what happened? Why didn't you come to the play?" Stuttering, Derron said, "Uh ... because I didn't want to." I went on to say that you could have just told me. By that time, the girl had noticed that him and I were talking and proceeded to come towards us. Before she could get too close, Derron stopped her and said, "I got this. Gone... I got this." Again he gestured for us to go outside of the church to talk so I followed him again. When we exited the church, Derron pressed his teeth together and said in a deep, but menacing voice, "Who the fuck told you to come to my church!" Looking shocked by his reaction and I said, "Baby, I just came to church because I was late for my service but still why you didn't come to my play? I paid $27 dollars for those tickets and baby you could have just told me that you weren't coming." The girl came out of the church door entrance and confronted me asking me why I was talking to her man. I said to her in responded by saying that if he was your man, he wouldn't have been with me on Wednesday." I went on telling her that I had no beef with her and that this was between Derron and I. Derron went back inside the church and the girl stayed outside trying to question me about my man/her man. Asking me when, who, what, what time, how, and why. I really didn't have much to say to this girl, but I remembered telling her three times that I had no beef with her and the situation was between Derron and me. About forty-five seconds had passed and Derron came back out of the door saying, "Fuck both of ya!" She quickly stopped arguing with me and ran behind him calling out him, baby. I became competitive and began calling him, baby and running behind him as well. For every one baby she called him, I called him baby two times and so on. The choir was singing and Derron flapped his long skinny arms and walked speedily through the church with both me and the girl behind him calling him baby, baby, sounding like two damn ducks squabbling over the same bread. An usher wearing a purple vest realized what was going on and began running behind all of us. My adrenaline pumped and at the same time I was trying to keep a little dignity by speaking low and ladylike. We all were making complete asses out of ourselves and with our highly, uncontrolled emotions we were all disrespecting God's house. The usher finally caught up with me and suggested in a caring, comforting way for me to come with her outside. I went with her, even to my surprise, because usually if I'm on to something or even after something, I don't give up or in until I get it. I guess you can say that the Holy Spirit had a hold of me even in the midst of that entire calamity. I went with the usher to the front of the church where all the craziness had started. She said to me, "Baby, it's going to be okay, let go and let God." I start trying to explain to her through my flowing tears and cracking voice that I was just with him and that we were in a relationship. I kept repeating myself and she replied, "Yes, I know, but it's not worth it." As she continued to speak, I became more composed and rational again to the point that I was able to listen to reasoning, especially because it came from a woman of God. Well... her talking to me was working and I was almost totally calmed down, until I just happened to look around and I saw Derron and the girl coming out of the side door of the church. Damn! I froze up in pain again and in that moment I started having flashbacks of the many times that I had caught Derron with someone and how I didn't do anything but stand like a deer caught in headlights. I guess he thought I was scary because he would always call me scary or a little white girl and even sometimes say that his female smoking buddies could whip my ass. Deep down inside I knew I wasn't the things he called me and that I could be aggressive if I choose to. But this episode pushed me to take a stand, yet it was just unfortunate that the stand had to have happened on holy grounds. Then again, I questioned if it was holy at all because of the behavior of the pastor there. Sadness and hurt once again filled my heart and made tears fall from my eyes. Without realizing it, I began taking off my jewelry one piece at a time. I took off my earrings, my necklace and then I instinctively dropped my cellphone and purse on the ground and took off running across the green pasture of the church, to where they actually had a cross posted on the lawn with a purple garment draped around it. I screamed out his name, "DERRON!" but he refused to acknowledge my voice from a distance and continued to walk alongside the girl through the parking lot.

When I caught up with him I was almost out of breath and began to repeat over and over to him, "Derron, we need to talk! This is not about her, it's about me and you." This continued for the duration of the walk, which lasted for about a minute. Once we arrived at her car in the parking lot, Derron began whispering to her regarding me, and he spoke loud enough for me to hear him but I still couldn't make out exactly what he was saying. They stopped at the car and I continued talking to Derron saying that we needed to talk. When I unexpectedly heard him say, "Get her!" I was so focused on him that it didn't register to me exactly what he was telling her to get. I kept right on talking to him when it hit me like a tone of bricks. I stopped dead in the middle of my sentence and said to myself, "Get me?" as if I couldn't believe what I thought I had heard. I looked at Derron and said, "You told her to get me?" I repeated this time to him and then quickly I turned to her and said in disbelief, "You really going to get me?" She gave no response but proceeded to walk towards me. I stood there and I did not move, yet I had no fear for my life or safety, because I thought I made myself clear to her earlier that I didn't have any beef with her. She got so close up in my face that she could have kissed me. That's when I realized that this shit was serious and I need to make a move. What move? I didn't know because I had no intention of fighting this girl. My reflex kicked in and within two seconds I had grabbed her neck and begin choking the life out of her. She was in a matrix backbend position and hung there lifeless. However, what was so strange about this is that while I was choking her, she couldn't lay her hands on me. Her arms dangled lifeless in mid-air, as if something or someone was holding her down, but she wasn't on the ground at all. I couldn't hold her up because she was taller than me. It was very strange. While I was choking her, I looked at Derron and saw evil in his face over her head. He stood with his arms folded and legs open wide watching me choke this girl out. He looked as if he was shocked that I was whipping her ass, or that he was getting off on two females fighting over him. I looked at him in disappointment, saying to him inside my mind, "Are you going to stop me from choking this girl the fuck out?" He wasn't stopping this one-sided fight and I soon realized that she was still dangling lifeless in the grip of my hands. Derron continued watching and looking like a pimp with a devil's advocate mentality that had no care or regard for neither one of us. Shortly thereafter, I felt someone jerk me around my waistline. One of the ushers had run down the hill from the church to try and pull me off the girl. When he couldn't break my grip from her, he literally had to peel my fingers off around her neck. Once he had successfully got me off her, she was able to grab a hold of my hair. I noticed that Derron was still not trying to help this beat-up girlfriend of his. The male usher held me until they picked her up off the ground and placed her in the car. When the usher released me I ran around the car to try to get at her again screaming, "I will kill you bitch!" Chasing after me, the usher was able to grab me again and that's when I started feeling pain in my right hand. When I looked at it, my middle finger was swollen as big as my big toe. Derron and the girl drove off and I witnessed my man of three years drive off and leave me there. I was so hurt that I began crying again because I couldn't believe what had just happened and not only that, I had told her over and over I didn't want to fight her. I proceeded to my car when the Dekalb County Police drove up. My heart raced and the words, "Oh shit I'm going to jail", went through my head. Thinking fast on my feet I felt I had to go into character as if this were a stage play in order to get myself out of this bind. Since my feelings were real for Derron I had no problem breaking that fourth wall and acting out my feelings to the police. When he approached me I was already crying so hard that I could hardly talk. I looked like Tammy Faye Baker with my makeup running from my eyes. The police tried calming me down, yet I continued saying in a poignant, but cracking voice, "I was just with him! I was just with him!" As I cried, I smeared my face all over his clean smoky gray uniform and my makeup turned his uniform a darker shade of gray. I fell to the ground and I could feel his strong arms trying to hold me up. I then heard his deep voice tell me over and over that it was going to be alright." I knew then that he felt my pain and his heart had gone out to me. Even after I had jacked his uniform with my makeup, the officer walked me to my truck and put me in it like I was a damsel in distress. He looked at me and asked me if I was okay. I nodded my head as I dried my face with some tissue I found in my truck. He then told me to leave the property and that I wasn't allowed to return.

Later on that day, Derron call me from a blocked number to ask me sarcastically how I did feel now. I responded yelling, "Bitch, I feel fine! You told your bitch to get me and she got- got!" You never know your strength until you have to use it when forced. Later on that evening my cousin, Tonya and I hooked up and went to Centennial Park to have a picnic.

CHAPTER 20
PUSHED BY FORCE

The month of June was about to roll in and I was trying to piece together the parts of my life, and my dignity in who I was as a woman and what I stood for and would no longer tolerate any longer. I was opening my eyes and taking off the fuck-fo-culars to actually calling a spade, a spade. Although I felt hurt and betrayed my anger was what carried me into another dimension of freedom that I called, "Be who you be." What that phase meant to me was that if you are a hoe, be the best hoe you can be and if you are maid, be the best damn maid you can be.

For years I'd tried to be someone I wasn't. After leaving a marriage that was abusive and controlling I decided to turn over a new leave and become submissive. Never again fight against anyone who was fighting me. Whether he was right or wrong I just wasn't going to fight anymore. Even though when I was all alone I was an aggressive, outgoing, and had a make it happen, get results attitude. I valued my own opinions, thoughts, and morals. I nearly gave up all of me just to be loved by someone who couldn't possibly give me something that wasn't in him; which was love. So I figured that if I had to start over it might as well be today.

I hung out more with my friends and met new people along the way. As weeks went by I became better at liking my own company again. I was alone but I was far from being lonely. My friends were always checking on me and making sure that I didn't slip into another depression. After not hearing anything from my Derron I felt that he had moved on and that he no longer wanted any part of me. I started getting strange calls from and unidentified number and when I answered the phone the caller would just hold the phone and listening to me. There were moments when I felt that the caller could have been Derron, but after thinking about for a second I would tell myself that it was just the wrong number.

One evening my girlfriend, Stephanie called me and invited me to go motorcycle riding with her and some friends. "I would love to," I told her and began getting dressed. "Ok, we'll be there in twenty minutes," she said. When they arrived, there were six bikers and only three of them had women riding with them. Stephanie introduced me to everyone, and then she showed me the guy that I was going to ride with. "Hi sweetheart, my name is Micah. How are you?" he said. After carefully looking him over I answered," I'm good, but I think you should know that I've never rode on a bike before so I'm new at this." Micah and everyone laughed and then he gave me some instructions as to how to ride with him and I got on the back of his bike. We headed towards the interstate to go to Dave and Buster's in Gwinnett. The night was beautiful and the stars were out. Riding on back of the bike gave me a sense of total serenity. The experience was totally arousing because I was gripping him tightly around his waist and ironic enough, he wore the same kind of cologne the Derron use to wear. When we arrived at Dave and Buster's we hung out in the parking lot and one of the biker's sisters was the manager there, so she had a waitress bring us food outside for us. It was going on midnight, and I was getting tired. "Steph, I'm about ready to go home. I'm tiredd and I don't want to go to sleep on the back on the bike and fall off," I said, stretching and yawning. "Shit, girl you're going to have to take a cab home because we're going to be here for a minute" one of the bikers said as everyone laughed. Micah came over to me and said, "Don't worry about them, I'll take you home and come back." When they heard him say that, everyone seemed pissed off, so they put on their helmets and got on their bikes. "Let's roll," Micah yelled out and we left. We pulled up to my house at 12:30 am and I got off the bike and said goodbye to everyone, but they didn't want to say anything to me so I went to my apartment. As soon as I put the key into the door my phone started ringing. It was an unidentifiable number so I pressed the ignore button on the phone and then Stephanie walked me inside. "Seneca girl...

that the guy you rode with wants to get to know you better." Stephanie exclaimed. "Uh, No thanks Stephanie, I'm trying to heal from this bad relationship I just got out of."

"Heal? Child Please! You will never heal by trying to save your pussy for him and he ain't even thanking about your ass! Seneca, he is out there getting plenty of pussy while you're here stuck on stupid. I'm here whenever you need me, but right now … I'm out." I thanked her and told her that I had a nice time. I watched as she walked out of the door shaking her head and seconds after the door closed, I heard her yell to her friends, "Let's roll." They cranked up their motorcycle engines and left.

The following week Stephanie called and told me that a major promotional event being held tonight in Buckhead and then she asked me if I wanted to go. When I was just about to answer her, she interrupted me and said, "Look Seneca, I almost gave up on your ass last time, but you are my girl that's why I'm trying my luck on you again. Don't come with any stupid shit, alright!" I smirked and said, "You got my word, Steph. I'm down with you." Although I was cynical, I felt I owed her a make up from the last invite so I got dressed for the occasion. When we arrived at the lounge in Buckhead and the place was crowded with many important people with titles and I wanted to intermingle with as many of them as I could. I definitely had my mind, heart and eyes open to meeting someone since Stephanie had called me out and checked me on my antisocial behavior. I went into the restroom to give myself a pep talk. I would often give these self talks just so I wouldn't get caught up in the hype of things. I was taught to always have an objective and my objective was to meet someone who was similar to my ex. Unfortunely I looked for guys that had Derron's his height, hair, complexion, or intellect, but the bonus that was absolutely mandatory was the need for him to have a big dick. The chosen one had to have at least two out of four plus the dick size in order for me to call it a, Go. I was going to go with what felt right and if the guy could first make love to my mind, then he would be the one. Stephanie and I mingled through the crowd and I spotted a prospect. Well, I believe we spotted each other. He was about 6'7" with a short haircut and a medium brown complexion and well dressed with about size 15 in shoes. I instantly thought to myself, "Hmm… this is the one."

I smiled at him as he walked towards me then he stopped. Looking down at me he said, "What's up, Ms. Lady? You are looking lovely tonight. What's your name?" I looked up at him and said, "Thanks, I'm Seneca… and yours?" He paused for a second and and then said, "Oh I'm sorry you just remind me of someone… My name is Chance." I laughed and looked away shaking my head. "What's wrong?" he asked. "Did I say something wrong?" he continued in a worried tone. "Oh no, you didn't say anything wrong. It's funny because you remind me of someone also." I replied. He asked me if I would like to go sit and talk, so Chance and I founded a table and began getting acquainted with each other. Stephanie came over and I introduced them, and then she whispered in my ear that she had to leave because of an emergency. I told Chance that I had to leave because of an emergency. He asked me if everything was ok and I told him yes and that I will call him tomorrow. We exchanged numbers and then Stephanie and I left.

When we finally talked again it was about three weeks later. I didn't want to look desperate and call him so I waited. When he called me, he told me that he had been out of town and asked me if I would like to go to dinner. "I would love to," I replied and we made plans to go to dinner that Saturday evening. When Saturday came Chance picked me up at 8:00 pm and we went to a very fine restaurant in Dunwoody. We told him a little about my life and kids and he shared to me that he didn't have any children and that he was a part-time college student working on his master's and he was also a full-time loan advisor. After we finished eating, he asked me if I would you like to come back to my house for a while?" When I heard this, my heart skipped a beat because to me that was a little more intimate than just dinner. I had to remind myself that I was single now, free, and had open options to be with another man in whichever way I pleased. In a soft tone, I answered,"Sure, that's cool." We left the restaurant and head over to his plad. When we arrived at his apartment, and when we got inside I looked around to check out his up-keep, and then I complimented him on his place. "Oh thanks baby. Would you like something to drink?"

"No, baby I'm good," I said, taking off my jacket. As I sat down on the sofa I thought to myself, "Hmm… this guy just might do."

Suddenly I heard Chance calling my name,"Seneca, Seneca!" He was calling me as I daydreamed, but I didn't hear him because I was caught up in deep thoughts about him. When I finally realized that he was calling me I said, "Oh, uh? I'm sorry baby I didn't hear you. I was thinking about something." He laughed then said, "I was going to tell you that I need to send a project by email to my professor and it's going to take a few minutes but I will be done shortly. Make yourself comfortable... ok? If you want to you can go into the bedroom and watch TV until I finish." I got up and proceeded towards the bedroom as he worked on some school stuff. I sat on his bed and turned on the television to look at the news.

About twenty minutes later he came in the room and bent over and kissed me. I was surprised and stimulated at the same time. When he finally let me up for air and he turned and then walked away while pulling his baby blue polo sweater over his head. I saw every single detail of his well-toned body. Now this was unusual for me, because I had never been the type to sleep with a guy on the first date, but Chance and I had been talking for at least a month so I made an exception to my rule. I knew what I wanted him and I had put myself in the right position. It had been a while since I had made love and I really needed the touch of a man. I was willing, ready and able so I took my clothes off and got underneath the sheets in his bed. Chance started coming towards me unbuckling his belt and unzipping his pants. I waited anxiously and with anticipation to see and feel his wood. He took off his pants and jumped into bed because it was so cold in room that it was freezing. Laughing at him, I pulled back the sheets so that he could land directly on his target... Me. Our body temperatures soon heated up the room and before I knew it we were kissing so fervently and he was sucking my breasts with gentleness. As he climbed on top of me and pressed his hard, sweaty body against mines. I reached under him to grab his wood to guide it inside of my walls. I received a big shock because his dick was so skinny and fairly small in length that I had a hard time trying to point it in the right direction. I thought to myself, "Damn Sen, you sure have done a physical feel on this guy because your feelings were off a bit." I felt the tip of the dick covered with a condom when he attempted to break inside of my walls. But he didn't have to try hard because his jewel was so damn small that it fit like needle in a haystack. Damn, he's finally in, I thought to myself and rolling my eyes. He started stroking and stroking until my pussy became somewhat wet and my legs spreaded further apart. I began working my hips to help with the process of his grand opening. However, after about two, maybe three strokes I all of sudden start seeing visions of Derron inside my head. I opened my eye quickly and said under my breath, "What the hell I'm I doing?" Chance thought I was whispering sweet nothings to him and said, "Yeah baby I know it's good." I almost said, "Nigga please…with this small ass dick?" But instead I moaned a little to play it off, then suddenly a tear streamed down my face and I began crying out to him saying, "Stop Chance. Stop! I can't do this," as I put the palm of my hands in his chest to stop him from going back inside of me. He looked at me with sweat rolling down his face and said, "Why are you crying baby?" He kept trying to slide his dick back into my pussy. "Look, I can't do this! I thought I was over my ex but I'm not and I'm sorry to have misled you," I said crying as I twisted and turned my body, maneuvering to get him up off of me. Chance sat up and said, "Damn, man why you played with me?" I didn't answer him and then I got up and proceeded to put on my clothes as fast as I could. When he stood up, he pulled the condom off and threw it on the floor and said, "You wasted my motherfucking time!" as he walked out into the living room. When I was finished dressing I grabbed my purse and went into the living room where he was sitting naked on the sofa with the remote control in his hands flipping through the channels. I looked at him and he was pissed off and stiff as he sat there. I was a bit timid to go sit next to him, so I stood in the doorway and told him that I hadn't meant to tease him but I wasn't as ready as I thought I was. He wasn't trying to hear anything I had to say so he got and went back to the room to get dressed. When he came back out I was standing by the door. "Oh… you are ready to go, I take it?" I answered by nodding my head yes. Chance grabbed his keys off of the countertop and we headed out the door.

While he was driving, I tried talking to him about the situation, but he was nonresponsive until we reached my house. When we arrived and my house, I exited the vehicle quietly and said thank you for the dinner; then I went inside. He drove off so fast that he nearly ran over my foot. After that night I didn't hear from Chance ever again and that when I began to I realized that Derron still owned my heart and my body obviously still belonged to him as well. I decided to put off dating and going out for a while and started staying around the house thinking about where my life was heading. I really loved acting and modeling so I decided to go so I sign up for acting classes to get my mind off of Derron.

One morning I began receiving the anonymous calls again. The person must have called at least fifteen times before I picked up the phone. In my heart I felt that it was Derron so I began telling the caller that I missed him and that I was still here when he was ready. Shortly after, the caller hung up and did not call back for about two weeks.

After leaving my acting class one night I thought I saw the girl that Derron was dealing with car parked in the back of my apartment complex. It was dark so I didn't pay it much attention and went into the apartment. About fifteen minutes after I got into my apartment someone called me from an unidentified number. "I'm sick of this shit," I said out loud so when I answered the phone, I sounded very upset and aggravated and shouted, "What!" The caller quickly hung up and the next morning around 6:00 a.m someone rang my doorbell. It scared me because I didn't have company so it was definitely unusual. I went to the door and said, "Who is it?" and a deep masculine voice answered, "It's me, open the door." I stutteredered and said, "Uh… hold on please" as I ran to the bathroom and brushed my teeth. I go back to open the door and there Derron stood with a red hoodie thrown over his head, his hands in his pocket. "What's up?" he said in low voice as he walked in. I shut the door behind him and walked towards my bedroom. I sat on the bed very quiet and waited for him to speak. He came and sat next to me on the bed and looked at me and said, "Seneca, I'm sorry for how I've treated you. You didn't deserve it." When he finished talking I was speechless. Not because it was what I wanted to hear, but because he had never apologized or take accountability for anything. So when he did apologize to me, I knew he meant it. I looked at him with tears in my eyes and told him that I forgive him. Immediately after, I excused myself to go to the bathroom to take a shower. Derron was undressed and lying on the bed when I came back into the room. With no time wasted, he called me over to the bed and told me to lie down. I said, "Hold on baby, let me put my clothes on." He instantly stood up and grabbed my arm pulling me towards the bed. As I climbed up on the bed he came from behind me and stuck his long tongue up my pussy, and he then flipped me over and spread my legs as far as east is to the west and then buried his face right between my legs. He started sucking my pussy as if he was trying to perform CPR on it. I clenched and grabbed the bed sheets because of the intensity of the pleasure; I was in an uproar. As much as I wanted to I couldn't hold back telling him how much I missed him and needed him to fuck the shit out of me. It seemed like the more I talked, the harder his dick became. Shortly after my pussy was breathing again from the CPR he performed. He layed back on the bed and waited for a return on his contribution to my now-wet pussy which I called, reaching my zenith. It was another way of saying, Daddi you're making my come." I crawled up between his well-toned hamstrings and pulled his dick towards my mouth as if I was pulling a handle of slot machine in Las Vegas trying to get lucky. As I covered the head of his dick with my mouth I could feel it jumping. I whispered, "Not yet, Daddi" just before I deep throated his Mandingo, chocolate dick. I must have sucked his dick for at least thirty minutes or more. This time around he started talking and nearly passing out from the erotic blowjob that I was performing on him. When he came, I thought that it was going to be a wrap and he would be ready to smoke a Newport but to my surprise Derron flipped me over and laid some wood right between my sugar walls. He left nothing to chance; he began sucking my nipples as he slid his dick in slowly. I was conquered, but by choice and I threw in the white flag and surrendered to his make-up of pleasure. He made love to me like he has never made love to me before. He stared directly into my eyes with passion and desire pouring out of him.

Afterwards Derron rolled over and reached into his pants pocket to get his pack of Newport cigarettes. I picked my cellphone up off the nightstand and it was going on noon then I laid back and stared up at the ceiling thinking about how good the dick was and that I didn't want it to end every again. "Baby, I got to go take care of something, but I'll be back later on tonight. Is that cool?" he said getting up off my platform bed. I sat up and puzzling replied, "Yeah, I guess so. If you must, you must but what time are you coming back?" He put his cigarette out and answered, soon. I looked up at him frowning and told him that he had to give me a time because I was not going to wait all night for him. "I'll tell you when I get out the shower," he said grabbing his clothes. While he was in the shower I got up to look out the window, and then it dawned on me that he hadn't signaled for me to finger him in his ass. It really must have been a little freaky thing at the time and now he was over it, I thought to myself. I was so relieved about that and was definitely ready to try to move forward with him, if possible. I was so deep in thought that I didn't hear him get out of the shower. When he came up behind me and said,"I hope you were thinking about me over there, while you daydreaming out the window and shit," I jumped and said, "Shit. You scared me! Yes as a matter of face I was thinking about you, but that's between me and God." He smirked and began putting on his clothes. I got back into bed and then he stooped over and kissed me and said, "See you tonight." I threw up a peace sign to him and then rolled over to go to sleep. He let himself out and locked the door behind him.

I woke up around 6:00 pm and I went to take a bath. While I was bathing I heard the phone ringing, so I wrapped a towel around me and went to answer it. Before answering it, I looked at the caller id and saw that it was Belinda. "Shit! What does she want?" I said in an aggravated voice. The phone rang five times before I picked up. "What up girl?" Belinda shouted as music played in the background. I wasn't going to tell her that Derron had been over, because she was going to say something negative which was more than likely the truth and I didn't want to hear. "Oh nothing…. Just chilling," I grumbled in a low voice, talking as if I had just woken up. "I wanted to see if you wanted to come to this party my friend is having up at the club." I replied, "Thanks girl, but I'm going to stay in tonight." Belinda started laughing and said, "What did you say? I didn't hear you. I put the phone down for a second." I was more irritated by this time and I answered, "No, I'm good." Belinda must have moved to another room or outside because I could hear her clearer than when she'd first called. "Look Seneca, I truly hope you ain't waiting around to hear from that Derron. You need to move on with your life, but if you change your mind call me." I didn't respond and just listened to her shaking my head. I then quickly interrupted and said, "Ok Belinda, I gotta call you back" bye," then hung up. As soon as I hit the end button on my phone a message popped saying that I had one new voicemail message waiting. I checked my voicemail and it was a message from Derron asking me to pick him up some Newport cigarettes and beer. I ran back to in the bathroom to finish my bath, and then I put on my clothes and headed to the gas station to pick up his items. While I was out I picked up some hot wings from Frankie's Bar and Grill just in case he wanted something to eat. It was close to 8:00 p.m when I arrived back at home. I cleaned up and turned on the radio and then I lit a couple of candles in the bedroom. I was in so much anticipation of a great evening with Derron that I vowed to myself to give him the 3B's when he arrived. The 3B's stood for Backrubs, Blowjobs and Breakfast in bed if he stayed the whole evening. It was a regular part of the routine before him and I broke up. My doorbell ranged and I yelled out from the bedroom, "Use your key!" because I that it had to be Derron. The doorbell continued to ring until he began banging on the door. I ran to the door and open it and Derron stood there with a cup in his hand looking very impatient. I smiled at him and asked him why he didn't just use his key. He walked past me through the door and headed to the kitchen. "If I knew where it was, I would have," he answered sipping on whatever was in the cup. I walked behind him and told him that his beer was in the fridge, his hot wings were in the microwave and his Newport's were in the bedroom. He turns to me and said, "Good looking out, baby." That was his way of saying that he appreciated it, or thank you. He grabbed his wings out of the microwave and went to the living room to eat his wings. I brought his beer out to him along with a frozen, ice-covered glass that I kept in the freezer. For about forty-five minute he sat down and watched basketball, as he ate and dranked. I waited for him to finish, and then I went to the bedroom. "I'll be in the bedroom Daddi when you're done." I kissed him on the neck and went into the bedroom. He came back about fifteen minutes later, only to find me waiting under the sheets. "Damn, baby you didn't waste any time …Uh?" he said as he began taking off his clothes. "Whatever." I replied turning my head away from him smirking. He got in bed behind me while I had my eyes closed and then I felt the stiffness of his dick touch my ass. My breathing became loud and rapid to the point that I had to pace myself just so I wouldn't hyperventilate. I grabbed his dick and began massaging the head of it between my thumb and index finger. I was ready for round two and there was nothing between us but air and plenty of opportunity. Suddenly Derron got up as if like he was going to get out of the bed, but instead he sat on his knees on the bed. As I lay there watching him; I thought that he was waiting for me to get up and turn my ass towards him, so that he could hit it from the back doggy style. But when I got up to turn around he laid down on his stomach. I looked on in confusion wondering what the fuck he was doing. It must be a new position that we're going to try, I thought. He spread his legs and reached around to grab my hand and then pushed it towards his ass. I just know he's not gesturing me to do what I think he is, I said to myself staring down at the back of his head. "Seneca, come on you know what to do for daddi" he muttered. He then pushed his ass in the air. I couldn't believe it, then again yes the hell I could. Sure enough, I had thought that part of his life had faded out away. Without saying a word, I slid my finger in and out of his ass and at the same time I was frowning and thinking that there had to be something a little more than what met the eye with this fingering bullshit. After all the fucking, sucking, licking and sticking we had done, I couldn't believe this motherfucker had the audacity to still want a finger up his ass! His cellphone began to ring so he told me to hold up for a second, and then he got up to look at the caller ID. "Umm… that's just Kenar. I'll call him back later," he said putting his phone into his pants pocket. He was getting back into bed, when I excused myself to go to the restroom. "Hurry back and get on Daddi's dick," he moaned as he stroked his dick up and down with his hand. I smiled and I said, "Keep it hard, Daddi," as I hurried away. In the bathroom, I washed my face and hands and then I sat on the floor. "I got to find out what's the deal with him tonight. If he is bisexual or gay I need to know," I repeated over and over to myself. When I returned to the bed Derron was still stroking his dick and motioning for me to go and sit on it. I stood over him on the bed, and then I squatted down right in his face making him suck my pussy until I came. Derron was so excited by now that he was stroking his dick faster and faster. I moved his hand out of the way and slid down on his dick and began riding it. It was going up and down, in and out, talking and popping all at the same time. "You like that don't you Daddi?" Derron looked on with glazed eyes as he began biting and sucking on my bottom lip. "Don't you come yet… and I mean it!" I moaned aggressively as I grasped the headboard and was breathing so intensely. Sometimes the pace would be fast and then he would slow down but all in the same the unyielding pleasure was long lasting. We were talking foul to each other the whole time, when finally he said something that gave me an open door to start my inquisition on his sexuality. Derron was about to come when he began breathing hard and murmured, " Baby, I want you to sleep with a woman." Although I had planned to go with the flow to find out about him, I was still offended by him asking me to do such a thing, but put my personal feelings aside and played my role. In a soft pleasurable voice I answered, "Oh yeah baby. Sure… I'll sleep with a woman, but first I want you to sleep with a man." Then I swallowed hard and waited for his response. I knew I was encouraging him to come out the closet, so I felt that what I was doing was right because I did not want to leave him unless I knew for a fact that he was gay. I started kissing his neck trying to cover my face just in case he wanted to slap the fuck out of me. To my displeasure, Derron began breathing harder that I could feel his stomach going in and out even though I couldn't see it. He responded saying a slow deep, deep voice, "For real, baby? Wouldn't that make me gay?" I answered, "Well, would it make me gay if I slept with a woman?" He said, "No." So I said, "Then, Of course not, Daddi." We had sex until two in the morning and then we fell asleep thereafter.

Derron woke me up around 5:00 am and told me that he was leaving. He kissed me on the forehead and told me he would call me tonight, and then he left. I went back to sleep but when I woke up I was thinking about what Derron had said about me sleeping with a woman and how he responded when I told him to sleep with a man. After about three hours of sleep, I got up and headed to work, but my thoughts were continuously on finding out about him during my whole workday. I even looked up information on the Internet to give me an insight on what to look for in a down-low or a homo-thug. I talked to friends about it, but I didn't tell them it was Derron I was speaking about. I decided to come up with a game plan that would really make him reveal himself…

CHAPTER 21
AN OPEN CAN OF WORMS

Derron began to open up to me more since that night. He was coming over but still leaving in the middle of the night and never really revealing what was up with him and that girl I had choked out at church. Although it bothered me I didn't ask about it because one way or another I was going to find out what was up with him and I had a mission and I needed to stay focused. Sometimes we would go to dinner and to the movies, but mostly we stayed at home to dine in and watch TV and have sex. Our sexual conversation was on a different level now. While we would be havin sex and Derron would say things like "Yeah, baby I know you want to see me put this big dick up a nigga ass. I would fuck the shit out him and have him begging for me to stop." I had to constantly remind myself that I was playing a role to find out information that he would tell. I never thought that I would hear this coming out of any so-called straight thug's mouth, not to mention … my thug. This shit was hard as hell to hear and stomach but in order to build my case on him I endured his sick talk. The number one reason I did this is because I was in love with him and didn't want to leave him, so I was looking for a strong enough reason to leave him alone and just maybe this could be it. I fell in love with a thug named Derron, not this questionable homo-thug. However, I was already in love with him and I couldn't possibly stop loving him just like that. I felt if I could just have stopped; then perhaps I never really loved him in the first place.

Every week more and more was revealed to me about him. Finding out about Derron had me scared for my girlfriends that were out there dating these thugs, players, pretty boys. I really was curious to know just about how many men like this there were in Atlanta, so I did a study to find out. One day I set up two personal ads with a free voicemail on a local chat-line. One of the ads were for a straight woman looking for a straight man and the other one was for a straight woman looking for a bisexual, young black male who would sleep with a bisexual thug. That evening when Derron came over I told him about this chat-line and said that plenty of guys were interested in coming over to be with us. "Well, when are you going to get a woman to sleep with?" he asked smoking his cigarette and watching the Louisville Cardinals play basketball on TV. "Umm... baby, we're going to get to that but let's just get to you first... ok?" I murmured while giving him a back massage.

Later on that evening, we went into the bedroom and began having sex. Derron started asking me questions about the chat-line and how it worked. I started explaining it to him and before I could finish explaining he interrupted me and told me to call the chat-line. When I checked the voicemail messages for the bi-sexual male ad, there were ten messages waiting. We listened to them together and I could see Derron getting turned on by listening to all the young black men and thugs ranging from the ages of 19 to 34 leaving messages expressing how they would love to suck his dick, and how they wanted to be fucked him. Just as we were playing the last message an interruption came in over the voicemail. It said that one of the members of the chat-line wanted to talk to me right now and to accept I needed to press 3. Derron was lying on top of me while I was on the phone so he whispered in my ear, "Press three." I could hear my heart beat skipping paces as I reached to press 3 on the phone. Silence came across the room and I could hear Derron breathing as we waited anxiously for the guy to speak. Suddenly a man's voice said, "Hello, Hello." Derron nudged me and nodded his head, gesturing for me to respond. "Oh... hello" I said slowly. The deep-voiced man said, "What's up? My name is Shorty Red. So what are you up to tonight?"

I then responded by telling that my thug wanted to fuck him and then I told him that if he was ready to be fucked by my man... anything could be up." I whispered as Derron listened closely. The guy then said, "Listen up yo. I'll fuck you and your man can watch but I ain't fucking him, yo!" Before I could respond Derron told me to end the call, and then as soon as I pressed the pound sign on the phone, the interruption came back on the phone saying with excitement that I had someone else who like to talk to me and to press 3 to accept the call. I looked at Derron and again he nodded his head for me to accept the call. This time I was ready so I sprinted off and said," Hello, who is this?" The caller was trying to tell me his name but there was a lot of noise in the background. "Hold on, hold on let me get out of here," he yelled as he seemed to be walking towards the exit of a club. "Okay, can you hear me now?" he laughed. "Yes, I can, so what's up?" I answered. The guy sound very young and talked with street slang. "Sheed... you tell me. I'm down for whatever. I want to fuck you and your man, but I want to fuck him first... Is that cool?" the guy asked. Derron seem to have like what he was hearing because his dick started jumping. He nodded his head gesturing to me that he liked this guy. Lost for words I said "Ok, yeah well umm, what's your name and phone number and I'm going to call you back with the directions." At that time the guy seemed to be walking back into the room with all the music in the background. He shouted, "My name is Cederick and my number is 678-555-1222! Just keep it on the low Shorty when you call... alright?" and as I was getting ready to hang up I heard a female in the background asking him who he was talking to and then the phone hung up the phone. I couldn't believe what I had just heard. There are a lot of young black thugs out there like this that I see downtown, at the clubs and with girls, guys that have pants hanging off their ass and walking with a funny ... swagger. I looked at Derron and he was zoning out about that call. He was so turned on that he had started coming before he fucked me. My head was swimming by now but I continued to play my role. I was hoping that Derron wouldn't ask me to call the guy back and will luck of my side, he didn't.

As weeks went by I continued to gathered information on him and the more details I knew the more I degenerated into hurt and shame and awareness of man being truly a homo-thug. Everything seemed to be unraveling in my face, but Derron still seemed to have transformed back into a manly thug every time we finished having sex. I was confused because although he was opening up to me; he was still behaving like a hard thug that wore Curves cologne, cornrow braids, baggy jeans and Air Force Ones.

The next day afterwards, Derron came over and told me that we weren't going to do any of those sexual acts any longer and that it was all in being freaky and fun. I believe he had thought about his behavior and wanted me not to think that he was gay or on the D.L. I was understandably confused, but a little happy as well. Derron and I took some time off from seeing each for about a week, but we still talked on the phone every other day. I had begun putting the thoughts out of my mind about him being gay or bi, until the following week he came over and we were right back at it again. I think he was struggling with his identity and fighting against how he really felt about men. This time I decided to go a little further so I started seeing how he would respond to different things that I did to him. I put him in my bra, pants and some pink gloss lipstick and again, my so-called man liked it. I started thinking that if he was on the down-low that he was probably relieved to be able to come out of the closet without being judged. Perhaps he was like this all along and my eyes were so wide shut that I didn't see it.

When Derron had sex with me he would often describe how he was going to fuck a man and what kind of man he wanted. "I wanted to get a transsexual. That's a boy who dresses up like a girl." Obviously he must have thought that I didn't know what a transsexual was because he described it and furthermore I was curious as to how Derron knew so much about them. Fear started entering my thoughts for my health. I had opened up a can of worms that I couldn't possibly seal back close. Now I had to make a move to leave this relationship without feeling like I led him on. I was still in denial about Derron being a homo-thug, so I decided to do one more test to truly assure myself that I was making the right decision to leave him.

One evening I told him that I wanted to go to the sex shop to get some toys for us so when he arrived at my house, we drove over to sex shop. When we arrived and walked in, I slowed my pace down so that he could go in lead the way. I wanted to observe him in the store to see if he was scared or embarrassed to be in there.An article I read on the internet told me that down-low men knows their territories and if you watched and observed he would lead you to it. As I watched he went directly over to the sex DVDs' and stopped right in front of the transsexual section. I stood back and watched him for a second thinking and said under my breath that he seemed very comfortable in here and then I walked up to him and grabbed his hand and said, "Baby, come on get what you really want," while rubbing on his back. Derron walked over to the black gay men DVD section and picked out a DVD. When we were heading to the front to pay for it I noticed a big dildo strap-on hanging on the wall. I thought to myself hat this might just be the breaking point. The strap-on dick had to have been at least seven inches long and two inches wide. I decided to get it and when I took it to the counter I was humiliated, but I stayed quiet and paid for it. The cashier looked at me, then she looked up at him and I could see her biting her bottom lip just to keep from laughing her ass off. We left the store and went back to my apartment and he put on the video in the bedroom and got undressed. "I will be right back baby" I said as I left the room to the bathroom with the strap-on still in the bag. I stared at myself in the mirror and said, I can't believe I'm doing this, as I proceeded to put on the strap-on. When I looked in the mirror it looked like I was some kind of freaky individual. I shook my head and said to myself, "Truth by told at all cost." When I went into my bedroom Derron had slipped into my flower printed panty and bra set. He was so skinny that it just slid right up on him. When I saw him and inhaled, then exhaled and walked in smiling. Derron didn't notice me come in the room because he was watching the tape with black men fucking and sucking each other as he jacked off his hard, stiff dick. I kept on inhaling and exhaling so I wouldn't cry out. Just as soon I got to the bed he turned around and look at me. He was breathing really hard and almost drooling at the mouth. I didn't say anything and just layed on my back on the bed with the strap-on sticking straight up in the air. Derron leaned over and started sucking on it. He then stood up and slid the panties to one side of his ass cheeks. He turned his around towards me and opened his legs then squatted down over me and sat on the dildo. I watched in shame and hurt as my man opened his ass cheeks and guided this seven-inch long, two-inch wide strap-on dick up his ass. He worked the dildo by rotating his hips left to right, right to left. I thought I would vomit on myself as I squirmed while he tried harder make it fit it in. Finally he was moving up and down with ease. He went to work on the strap-on dick; riding it up and down. Groaning and Moaning filled the room as he pleasured himself. His manly groaning was horrifying because it sounded like a gorilla giving birth to a baby gorilla. Tears filled my eyes and every part of my soul and spirit screamed out that it was true and confirmed. Once he came, he got off of the dildo and layed next to me. I quickly wiped my eyes and got up off the bed and went back to the bathroom. I locked the door behind me and turned on the water; then I unstrapped the dildo off of me and it hit the floor. My tears that I had been holding in began flowing freely to the bathroom floor as I layed balled up in a fetus position because I became sick on my stomach. There was no other place to look, and no other excuses to make and no more denial that I could hide under because he had left me no choice but to leave. I felt betrayed, low and degraded as a woman and the dildo was still lying on the floor as the water ran. I kept my hand over my mouth to keep from crying out as I cried silently to the walls.

CHAPTER 22
TORN

It was the end of December and I tried to stay away from Derron as often I could I started deeply considering what to do about him and I. I knew deep down in heart that it was official and he was on the DL. Although he hadn't still come straight out and told me. I felt at this point it wasn't necessary because the proof was front and center. He had shown me not once, not twice, not three, not four but over five times that he was in fact homo- thug. I fought against the feelings I had for him and the cold hard truth that I now knew about his sexuality. The truth stared me in my face and wouldn't let me deny it any longer. I began to make up excuses not to see him so that I could try to find the strength that I didn't have to leave him. When he would call I would just answer the phone and pretend like I was busy by telling that I had an audition or a model's call to go to. Like I said, I didn't know how to tell him that I didn't want to see him anymore. After all this was the man that I left my husband for, so it wasn't easy. Besides we had history together and it just so happened that I was still in love with him. I didn't understand what I was feeling but I knew that I didn't want to judge him because I cared so deeply for him and his family. Sometimes I wondered if he had always been this way and I was just too blind to see it or if he had got turned out by someone out in the streets.

One afternoon my sister, Phoenix called me to see how I was doing. She knew about the whole situation of what had gone on between Derron and I. "Seneca this is a good for you to bring up that girl that he has been living with." she said. She thought that if I brought the subject up about the girl it would make him want to leave me alone just so it didn't have to explain himself. I was glad she had some ideas but for some strange reason, I was scared too. Phoenix started telling that I needed to put an end to this sick relationship with him and move on with my life. After giving it some thought, I agreed with here and decided that I would do it. When we hung up, I immediately called him and told him that I needed to talk to him. "About what?" he said trying to use an intimidating tone. In the past his intimidation usally was enough to make me back off, but I didn't care anymore. I started by telling him that I did love him but I needed to know where he stood with that girl. He became very offensive saying telling me not to question him. I run things and you don't, he added. He went on to say that the girl was only there helping paying bills and she would be gone in February of the next year." He began threatening me by saying that I better never step to him like this again or else he would cut me off. A part of me wanted to call that I didn't give a flying, fluke of a fuck what he did, but the other part of me couldn't believe he was trying to act like a man again. For weeks I didn't say anything else about it, but I still kept my distance from time to time and would just see him maybe once every two weeks. Christmas was approaching and a part of me wanted to be with him on Christmas, because I couldn't just stop loving him, even though I knew so much about his down-low lifestyle. One week before Christmas day I received a text message for Derron that reading "Merry Christmas, I'm out of town, see you next week." I read the text and in anger I threw the phone on the bed. I spent the holidays with family and friends, but I still possessed a kind of sadness because a part of me wanted to be with him and the other part wanted to leave him. After Christmas I spent the next week alone thinking about my life and learning to love myself again.

When Derron called he got a shock that he never thought that he would get from me. I told him that it was over between us and that he could have the girl, because I was done. I couldn't believe that I had said it but it was a feel-good moment for me because for once I had stood up to him. Two days later he called me from work, saying he wanted to talk to me. I was very cynical, but I said, "Ok… talk." While I waited for him to speak, I heard the intercom in background call for him to report to the front office. "I'll call you right back," he said racing off the phone. I hung up and continued on with my business.

Five minutes later he called back and when I picked up he just started talking. "Baby, listen I'm not ready to let you go. I won't let you go! I know I've fucked up with you but I do love you, but don't let it go to your head … And about that girl… man, that girl will be leaving soon I promise but I ain't letting you go!" I was stunned and speechless all at same time. I couldn't utter a word and tears streamed down my face as I stood outside on my balcony in the cold. "Seneca, did you hear me?" he yelled. Clearing my voice I answered, "Yes Daddi I heard you, I just believe what I'm hearing." He then said he would call me later and before he hung up the last words out of his mouth was I love you. I whispered back I love you too and just like that I was wheeled back in by those three magical words. "What's the fuck wrong with me? Why do I can't I leave this guy alone?" I continue asking myself over and over. I realized that will him it didn't take much for me because I all along all I wanted was for him to love and want me. Derron and I were back on again and I now realized that I was in love with a down-low thug and I felt that maybe if I just hid it from my friends that everything would be ok. I was in denial and knew the truth at the same time. "He couldn't possibly be; maybe it's that Gemini personality that got him so freaky," I kept to convince myself. The hard thug he showed me kept me in denial that he wasn't a bona fide homo thug. I was lying to myself and as it turned out I was now living in his world without realizing it I had become a part of his sickness. I loved him more than I loved myself, my family or friends. It was like he had a power over me. We continued having sex and the routine of the fingering his ass was still the main course as far as he was concerned. I knew it wasn't normal in my heart and I wanted to leave – but I couldn't. I would think about all the things he had done to and for me as a man and that would sometimes be enough to push everything out of my mind. I wanted him to change and I was hoping that this was a bad nightmare that I would eventually wake up from.

Later on I also found out that his church, the one I attended with him and got into a fought in was in fact a gay church. All this time, I had been going to a gay church with my man and didn't even know it.

One morning Derron and I went to the church that I had joined and this well-known pastor was there visiting during a conference for men. We went and the pastor called every man down to the altar so that he could pray over him for deliverance. Derron went down to the altar, but as the pastor began praying and laying hands on the men and they would fall down to the floor. I watched to see the pastor laid his hands on Derron. Astonishingly, Derron stepped back so that the pastor couldn't touch him. I was shocked and just kept praying for him in my spirit. After the service was over we went to the car and Derron had this scared little boy look on his face. His eyes were wide as if he had seen a ghost. I asked him what was wrong and he replied, "Baby that pastor was touching everybody and they were falling out. I didn't want that man to touch me." I grabbed his hand and said, "Baby that pastor is anointed by God and he was not going to hurt you. He is only going to help you!". I knew then that there was some darkness going on with his spirit that was not of God.

I went to church every Sunday after that because I knew what was in him was probably in me now because I had been told that spirits traveled through soul ties. I felt an urge to just hear from God, so I started going by myself so I wouldn't be distracted. Derron continued going to his church, but one Sunday, the same pastor came back to visit my church and I invited Derron to come with me. We had to go into the overflow room because the church for full to its' capacity. When this particular pastor was preaching, Derron and I were standing up holding hands and repeating what the pastor told us to repeat. "THE BONDAGE IS BROKEN! THE BONDAGE IS BROKEN!" the pastor shouted. As I repeated these words I heard Derron murmured something so I looked up to acknowledge him and he repeated himself. He looked down at me and said, "Ain't no bondage broken. I still got power over you," and smirked. I looked at him perplexed and dismayed and told him that he shouldn't say things like that. "Why did you say that?" I asked. He didn't answer and just turned his head back towards the projection screen that we were looking at in the overflow room and continued listening. I sat down and stared at my Bible. I started praying silently and I felt a strong need to seek God's face more than ever before because Derron had shown me that I was dealing with Satan himself in disguise.

When church was over I had very little to say to Derron. We arrived back to his house and I told him that I needed to pick up my girls from their grandmother's house, and then I left. As I drove home I thought about all the signs that had been right in front of me. There were warning signs I believe that God had sent me 3 years earlier. There were signs about Derron that I couldn't see because I was so caught up into being submissive to him and our sex. Now that I can see clearer, It now make sense to me that how we had to dress alike in the same colors when we went out and how he didn't look disrespect me by looking at other women. I thought it was because he loved me, but now I feel that he did these things because he was actually competing with me and didn't want me to stand out. Also, I now felt that he wasn't looking at the women because he was to busy looking at the men. I reflected back on the dreams and visions that I used to have about him and how they were trying to reveal to me Derron's true character. I thought about the dream I'd had when he was in the closet in my house trying on my ex-husband's clothes with a bright light above him. I felt God was trying to show me that he was covering up something that he was hiding and the light showed that it would one day be revealed. I reflected back on the two little boys that I'd dreamt about that my daughter was babysitting in that same dream. God was showing me the twin baby boys that I would have had if I hadn't aborted them. I also thought about the dream in which the lustful tongue was licking me from underneath my bed and I liked it, then I start praying and it released me. I felt God was revealing to me that in the midst of my sin… God was standing by me and that even though I was being controlled and ruled by Derron's sex, the only way out was to turn to God. Then to really push things over the top, I thought about the time when I fought at the church and Derron stood over that girl and I and watched us like he was the devil's advocate and provoked the fight on holy grounds. Every dream I had had regarding Derron had played out in a significant way in my life. I believed that it was God's way of forewarning me about my life and the unwise choices that I would make if I didn't heed the warnings. I was once told that when you get out of God's favor, he has a way of orchestrating your life to the point where he's your only hope for recovery. Even when God lets us know that he's not a part of our mess and the choices that we make for ourselves, he won't condemn us when we acknowledge our wrongs and turn away from them.

CHAPTER 23
OPT-OUT

"The cat is out of the bag" was a true saying that existed now in my life. I could know longer deny the truth that was in front of me about Derron. However, I remained in torment about completely leaving him, even after I became closer to God. It seemed as if my rights and wrongs were at war with each other. From time to time my mind would sway back to the unconditional love I had for him and for some reason or another I felt that he himself was hurting on the inside and I needed to be there when he fell to pick him back up. His confusion, anger, rage, and self-abuse made me feel that he needed me and was crying out for help through his behavior. Some of my friends said that I was still practicing denial and it was all bullshit, but it didn't matter because I wanted to help him. My pastor use to always say that hurt people, hurt other people and those they do it; do it to the people who care the most for them. I prayed for God to speak to Derron's heart and heal him, but he seemed to want nothing to do with God and everything to do with the world. When I would see him it was hard not to give in to his desires even though I now knew the will of God for my life. I couldn't be in his will, and be of the world to so I had to start making decisions about which I loved most God or Derron. I tried expressing myself to Derron about God and how I wanted to change but still be there for him. He didn't want to hear it and would still do what he wanted to do.

One Monday morning I woke up early in the morning and turned on my TV and a pastor was talking about relationships. He said something that morning that nearly changed my life. He said what you compromise to keep you will eventually lose anyway. When I heard him said this I instantly thought about all the sick sexual acts that I was doing for Derron just to keep him happy. I got out of bed and lay out on the floor on my face crying out to God with tears running down my face saying, "God, I don't want to leave him, please don't make me! I feel I'm being forced to leave someone that I truly love, perhaps more than he love himself. Please Lord don't force me to leave Derron!" I layed on the floor crying for about 2 hours and then I got up to take a bath.

Since that time, I started having dreams that I had HIV and that I was in surgery but they couldn't save me. Also I would have dreams of Derron being faceless. I couldn't understand the meaning of that dream, but I came to the conclusion that it couldn't have been good. I knew I had to make a choice to live and not die, because if I didn't leave, I would have more than likely ended up with HIV by having sex with him. These dreams were so vivid that it seemed like it had already happened. I began thinking about my life, my kids, my family, my career, and all the warnings God had given me. My life would have been wasted over my own desirers and lust for a man who didn't give a damn about anything or anybody but himself.

I called Derron on the phone and told him that we needed to talk in person. I was going to inform him that I was breaking up with him because I was afraid of catching AIDS. He agreed to come over to talk, but when he arrived I choked up. Derron sat on the sofa and said, "Ok, what did you do?" I had tears in my eyes and said, "I didn't do anything. I just want to tell you that I can't see you anymore." He looked at me with a smirk on his face and said, "Yeah right!" Then he grabbed me and lay on top of me, holding my arms down. "Baby look, I'm weak for you and I can no longer do what you want me to do!" I cried. Derron quickly kissed me on the lips and said, "Stay weak, stay weak," as he unzipped his pants and pulled my skirt up and tried to stick his dick in me. I closed my legs tight and said I had to go to the restroom. He then rolled over on to let me get up. While I was in there I prayed, "Lord, help me to be strong from the lust I have for Derron. Please cover me with your blood," as tears rolled down my face. When I returned to the bedroom, Derron was lying on the bed with my panties and bra on with pink lipgloss on his lips. "Damn not this again!" I yelled. He got on his knees and bent over, letting me know that he wanted to be fucked. He knew that I was in love with him and would do anything he told me to do, so he waited for me to strap on and fuck him. I pretended that my tooth was hurting and that I need to lie down. With disappointment in his eyes Derron got up and went into the closet where I kept the strap-on, then he laid back on the bed and put his legs straight up in the air and slid the dildo in and out of his ass until he came. When he finished he got up and pick up his jeans, his Tupac t-shirt and his black and white Air Force One shoes and went to the restroom to wash up. When I heard the bathroom door close and the shower come on I ran into the living room and began sobbing, but I covered my mouth with a towel so he couldn't hear me. I heard the shower turn off so I walked back to the bedroom and all I kept hearing in my mind was what you compromise to keep you will lose anyway.

Derron soon came out fully dressed looking like a thug again. Every time I saw him dressed like that it was so appealing to me. That is one of the reasons that kept me swaying back and forth about him. His phone rang and it was one of his homeboys calling. Derron answered, "What up folks? Yeah, yeah I'll meet you at the Mexican bar in College Park in about forty-five minutes," he said talking in a deep manly voice. "Alright Shorty, I'm going to hang out with my people. I'll call you tomorrow," he said as he kissed me on the forehead and grabbed his keys. I smiled and said ok as I walked up to him to the front door. I was really messed up in my head but I held my composure until he was out of there. I realized that he was not going to give up his sickness and although I had opened the can of worms or released the woman that was trapped inside of him; I had to change myself by leaving him this time for good but I didn't really know how.

When he left I ended up calling my father and broke down and told him everything. Although he was shocked, my father gave me very wise advice and told me to search for another apartment and start over my life. At first I agreed with him and then the other part of me kept saying that I didn't want to be without him no matter what. I knew I had to do this for three reasons. One was to save myself from catching AIDS. The other was I was born a woman and my man was trying to make me into his man and I wanted to feel like a normal feminine woman again. The third reason was that I knew now that in order to be in the will of God for my life, I had to be transformed by renewing my mind and the only way to do that was to give up my world and everything that was in it. I muscled up the strength through prayer, because I couldn't say no to Derron and I learned that anytime I tried to do something in my strength I failed. There was saying that said if you can't beat them, join them. I didn't want to join Derron's way of life so I decided just to run away from my weakness by starting my givng my life to Christ and dying to all the formal things.

I found an apartment about 25 minutes away from my old complex. Therefore, my kids didn't have to change schools and it still would take to long to get to work. The apartment approved me quickly and within one week I had moved out and changed my phone number so that Derron could never contact me again. I felt bad and it was really hard at first because it looked and felt like I had abandoned someone that I truly loved. It boiled down to me loving myself enough to leave him or becoming more entangled in the sickness of his true identity, which was his real life. My life was important and through Christ I realized that my life had a purpose and a plan that did not include Derron who had nearly taken me to my death not once, but twice. I had abandoned the relationship and cleansed my body, mind and spirit of all his homosexual behaviors and was now learning that I didn't have to give up my life just to be loved by him.

CHAPTER 24
BREATHING AGAIN

"Take one, aaand action!" the director shouted as he directed me in my first speaking role in the movie *Complex Union*. I played a character by the name of Tinese. Six months after leaving Derron, I ventured back out into the acting and modeling industry. It took a while for me to get back in the swing of things, because at times I would break down and have crying spells about the decision I made to leave Derron. I didn't have any interest in dating at all because I had nothing else to give to anyone. Derron had drained me mentally and physically and now it was about me pushing myself to get on with my life again. I had moved on with my life and decided that I was going to go full speed ahead with my modeling and acting career.

I also became heavily involved with the church by ministering to young women about not having sex and keeping God first in their lives. It was now important for me to bring awareness to sexual spirits that soul ties can take over your life through people that you get involved with on that level. I started an organization that informed young girls of the risks they would take if they had unprotected sex, but more so encouraged them to not have sex until they were married. I went into the clubs to get my message out there to young women who was not in church. I didn't try to stop the flow of the club, but I did mention to girls while they were in the restroom touching up their makeup or talking to each other. I hung out with my girlfriends from time to time at other nightclubs, parks, and sport bars, but I wasn't ready to allow them to convince me to talk to anyone else because for me it was about loving and being myself and making better decisions.

CHAPTER 25
STARTING OVER

My weekends began to revolve around my kids, church, going to the clubs with my girlfriends from time to time, and acting. I wasn't quite over Derron, but I knew in my heart that there was no way that I was going back him. I was learning how to love myself again and to get back into the world and live my life without compromising it again for any man. From time to time, I would have to drive through Decatur to get to my cousin's house, and I would think about Derron, but the memory of him was slowly disappearing from my heart.

After about two months; of getting settled in my new place I recieved a letter in the mail from the Fulton County health department. The letter stated that I needed to contact them as soon as possible. I was astounded and curious as to why I had received this letter. I wondered how the hell they get my address and then I looked at the bottom right corner of the envelope and saw that the mail had been forwarded from my old address. I hurried home to call the health department but after several tries I realized that it was almost 5:00 p.m and they were probably closed. I guess I'll call them first thing in the morning. I had no clues as to what it could have been about. Derron came to my mind and a clammy sweat began to form as I thought about why they were trying to contact me. I stared at the letter and continue to ponder on the reason. "But what if...? I would say as I debated back and forth with different what if questions. I couldn't have anything, it's just a routine letter" I said as I fought back and forth with the negative thoughts that passed through my mind. Later on that evening, I put the kids to bed then I went to lay down, but I couldn't sleep at all.

I continued to think about the letter and wanted very much to speak to the representative that had sent it to me. Turning constantly in bed and moving from one end to another, I decided to get up and pray as my pastor had taught me. I reached to get the letter off of the nightstand, and then I got my Bible and knelt beside my bed, saying to God, "Lord, according to your word, by your strikes my body is healed from all sicknesses and diseases. I rebuke every plan that Satan has for my life and I seek blessing and favor over this letter for I am healed. Lord, you said that there is no condemnation in Christ and I have been forgiven." After praying, I laid back down and repeated, "I trust God," over and over until I fell asleep.

The next morning after getting the kids to school, I call in to work and my boss that I couldn't come in today because I was sick. When I told my boss that; I had my fingers crossed because I hoping that I wasn't real sick after getting the letter. I decided rush down to the health department instead of calling. As I waited for the place to open at 8:30 a.m, I heard a voice tell me to be anxious for nothing, but through all things prayer and supplication. I began speaking out loud while looking out the window and said, "God must have known that I was anxious for this place to open.", then I smirked. M o m e n t s later I started seeing employees going into the building, but they still weren't open yet. Shortly after, the security guard pushed the door open and put the OPEN sign up in the window. I rushed out of my truck and ran inside the building. I had to stop at the security booth to be searched before entering the clinic. Rushing to the top of the stairs, my anxiety came back and I started repeating silently, "I trust God, I trust God." When I made it to the top of the stairs, there was a clerk at the window. I went over to her and said nervously, "Good morning, I received a letter saying that I should contact you, but I'm not sure what it's about." The clerk smiled and asked to see the letter. I reached into my purse and gave it to her and as she read it, I began praying inside my head. "Oooh… Ms.Martin, we sent this letter to you and basically it's a procedure we do to get you in to test for HIV." I felt a little relieved, but then I was still uncomfortable and confused as to why they sent it to me. Why are you contacting me? Who…?" Before I could finish my sentence she interrupted and said with a very serious demeanor,"This letter is sent to people who have had sexual involvement with a person who is HIV positive, but like I said, it's strictly procedure and it does not mean that you have it." I was stunned and couldn't say a word. A single tear came down my face and I began faltering, "Who… who is the person?"

The clerk came from around the desk where she sat and took me in the back to speak to a counselor. They gave me a hospital gown and told me to put it on and then I sat in the room in my white hospital gown, waiting from the counselor to come in. All kinds of thoughts ran through my head as I reflected on my kids, my family, my friends, and then my kids again. At the same time I knew I had to believe the word of God because I had been taught that Satan came to steal, kill and destroy and all three of those actions seemed to fit my situation at that time. I knew that no matter how I felt I had to confess the word of God and not be controlled by what I saw, heard or felt. I began confessing to God all over again in my head and then the counselors knocked on the door and entered into the room. "Hello, Ms. Martin. My name is Tawanda Miller and I'm going to perform a HIV test on you today, but your test results will not be back for about two weeks." I stood up and began questioning her. "Who gave you my name?" The counselor said that she couldn't share that information with me and continued to say that a sexual partner that I once had tested positive for HIV, and gave them my name as well as others. Now, do you have any other partners that you were sleeping?" I sat quiet for a moment then I answered, "Ma'am I don't! I've have only had one partner and we're no longer together." She couldn't give me his name, but I knew exactly whom she was talking about. She then smiled at me and said, "Ok good we can start the test right away. She also said that she was glad that I came in because there are a high percentage of black women dying of AIDS than any other race. She went on explaining to me about the virus and then took my blood for the test.

I left and went home and didn't mention it to anyone at all. I knew people had the habit of speaking negative and I just wanted to trust God's word so I did I didn't ask the counselor many more questions. I went on with my life as usual trying not to think about my situation, but sometimes I would wake up in the middle of the night crying uncontrollably. This went on for the whole two weeks and then it was time for me to go back and get my results of the test. I was nervous and anxious all over again, but I knew I had to know, so I raced down to the clinic.

When it was time for me to go back to talk to Tawanda, she came out nd got me from the waiting room and took me into a private office. I didn't wait for her to close the door behind us before I spoke out and said impatiently, "What are my results?" The counselor walked to the desk and sat down then she replied, "Hold on, Seneca. I have to go get the paper, ok?" When she was gone I paced the floor back and forth until she returned. Coming back into the room she smiled and said, "You're really ready to know... uh? I-.", but before she could finish her sentence I lashed out at her telling her that she would be fucking anxious too, if this was her going through this! You don't know the hell I've been through waiting at day and night to find how whether or not you're going to die!" She told me to lower my voice and then closed the door behind her. She went to her desk and said down and gestured for me to have a seat. Once I sat down she said, "Now, you wait just one minute now! I have been very professional and help to you, but since you want to get person with me, I'm going to call you by your first, Seneca! I understand that you are upset but I'm only trying to help you. I jumped up out of my seat and yelled, Help? How the hell is you trying to help me, you get paid for this! You care about me!" The counselore jumped up from behind her desk and yelled back. "How the do you know I don't care. Do you know my story? Do you! Well since you don't know let me tell you. Have a seat, Seneca! I began trying to talk and she yelled again, "Have a seat!" I sat down and looked up at her while she stood in front of me. She paused for a second then she said in a calm voice, "Seneca, I once made foolish choices too. I had with my boyfriend and I had sex with him without a condom and I choose to live a promiscuous life, having sex with whom ever I please as I said who, where and when. I interrupted her and told her that I have never done anything like that. She put her finger her lip and gestured for me to be quiet. "Let me finish, Seneca. I turned my head toward the windows and she continued. "You see I wasn't one of the luck ones that came out scared free, though. I had a good time out there in the streets but I was one of those girls who decision caused her to be infected with HIV. When I heard her say that word my heart skipped beats and I slowly turned back towards her and tears began to stream down my face. I tried to apologize saying that I didn't mean to be disrespect and that I was sorry. I then asked her if she was ok. She looked at and smiled and then said, "I'm ok. I'm dealing with it and I have been living with HIV for 5 years now." She got up and came over to me and laid the envelope on the desk where I sat. "Now, Seneca I'm here for you, but here are your results." I wiped my eyes and looked down at the envelope and began crying again. "Seneca, do you want me to read it?" she asked with empathy. I was quiet for about a minute, and then I nodded my head gesturing to her to open and read it. As she torn open the envelope and read the results as I clenched my purse. She looked up at me and said in a calm demeanor, "Seneca, your results are-are negative." I quickly grabbed the paper from her and looked very closely at it. It did in fact say that I was negative. I fell onto the floor and began crying and thanking God at all the same time. The counselor allowed me to stay there for about a minute, and then she helped me back into the chair. She was getting ready to start back talking to me when a nurse knocked on the door. The counselor told me to hold on and she got up to open the door. When she opened it the nurse asked her was everything ok. She told her that everything was fine and as she was closing the door back the nurse looked in and smiled at me. The counselor came back over to the desk and sat down; then she told me that she needed to now talk to me about protecting yourself. I dried my face and began listening to every single thing she had to say about prevention, condoms, and abstinence, and she urged me to continue being tested. She said that even with my negative results I still needed to get tested every six months. At this time, I was still in released and happy, yet dismayed because she was living with the diease and that God had again saved me from my sins and prevented the devourer from destroying and taking my life.

CHAPTER 26
SILENT EYES

The big birthday bash was coming up and almost half of Atlanta was getting ready to spring out in their best outfits to see the celebrities perform. Vanessa had bought two tickets from this guy on the street because the tickets were so expensive to buy at the box office. We went to the South Dekalb mall to find the perfect, sexiest outfit to wear. When we arrived at the mall there were men everywhere flaunting their Roca wear, Nikes Air Force Ones, Polo shirts and other name brand Gear. The mall was like a fashion show because if you weren't wearing the hottest and latest style you merely existed. I really didn't see the big deal in looking for guys who only wore name brand clothes. In fact, I wasn't looking to meet any guy no matter what he was wearing. I mean, even if he was dressed like Puff Daddy at a Grammy awards ceremony and had a dick bigger than the stack in his wallet I was still not interested. Especially after the scare that I had endured four months ago that could have ended up with me not even having the option to pick or choose who I wanted to do. The option to choose is what Derron almost took away from me, when he played Russian Roulette with my life. I know that I had chosen wrong when I decided to play a role in finding out whether or not he was gay. His dishonesty about his sexuality, and not to mention being in love with him, didn't help me to make a better choice, so he really left me no choice other than to investigate and to find out the truth on my own. I didn't mean to get involved so deep.

Vanessa and all my friends felt that going to the Birthday Bash would be good for me, since I had not been out for the last few months and they didn't know it but I was seeking a counselor to help me gain back the little dignity and self-respect that I had left. I had spoken with my therapist about it and she too thought that it was a great idea, but advised me to take my time and not to rush into anything.

Vanessa and I were walking through the mall laughing and just enjoying our day out, when she suggested that we go get something to eat in the food court. After getting our food she spotted one of Derrons' friend coming into the food court towards us. "Seneca, girl look, there's Derron's friend, Tyler." I quickly grabbed all my shopping bags on the table in front of me to cover my face and I peeked between the bags to look. "Seneca, what's wrong with you?" Vanessa asked laughing. I put my finger up to mouth and gestured for her to be quiet. Terrell was walking right up to our table smiling. "Ahh... girl don't even try to hide from me," Tyler said laughing. Vanessa laughed and then she hit me on my leg underneath the table. Just as I was about to respond to her painful but unexpected hit, Tyler sat down at the table. "Seneca! How have you been?" he exclaimed with excitement. "I'm well, thank you and you?" I cautiously replied not knowing what he was going to say next. "I'm good and I see you are looking good, too." But you've always looked good.", he said flirtatiously. I smiled and looked away. Vanessa started shooting the shit with him and talking about the clubs, old times and stuff like that. I didn't have much to say at all. This was Derron's friend and I didn't want any information to leak about my whereabouts. Tyler asked me had I you spoken to Derron lately?" My heart raced just hearing his name and I quickly shook my head no, then got up and excused myself to put away my food tray. As I looked back over towards the table I saw Vanessa talking to Tyler. I was concerned about what Vanessa was saying to him, because the way she ran her mouth I know that she would tell him where I lived without realizing it. Tyler then he got up and walked towards me and said, "Seneca for whatever it's worth I always thought you were good for Derron and treated him well. I can't believe he let you go; you seemed to be such a good woman." I looked at him in puzzlement and said, "What do you mean, he let me go?" Tyler looked at me flabbergasted and said, "Uh? You know Derron breaking up with you." I put my tray down and said, "Derron didn't tell you. Did he?"

"Tell me what?" he replied. "Well from my understanding, it was nothing to really tell. He said he had to leave you because you were fucking up on him. Isn't that what happened?" asked Tyler. I felt tears forming in my eyes and I hastily said to him, "No, that's not what happened, but it isn't my job to tell you anything. You're his friend ask him! I-I gotta go now." I began walking away from him and Tyler yelled out, "Seneca wait!" When I stopped he walked up to me and said, "Look, I didn't mean to upset you, but take care of yourself." Covering up my feelings and what I really wanted to say, I responded by saying, "Okay, but I'm good, sweetie. I just don't want to have shit to do with him and I don't want to hear anything about him. You take care too." Vanessa came over to me with our bags and asked me if I was okay, and then we left the mall.

While driving back to the house I questioned her about what she and Tyler were talking about. "Oooo… girl! He was just saying that Derron was in the hospital about two months ago and that he's doing better now. He told me to tell you but I told him that you probably wouldn't want to hear anything about him at all and that you were trying to move on with your life." In a shaken tone I said, "Hospital! Oh God is he ok?" Vanessa pulled over into a gas station and put her truck into park. "Yeah girl, that fool is fine. He said that he had a touch of the flu, but Tyler also mentioned that he thought Derron had started doing some cocaine because he had gotten skinner," she said as got out of the car to pump gas. While she was away, I started thinking about how Tyler actually thought that Derron was snorting cocaine, when in fact he had HIV positive. I started thanking God again for sparing my life and my health. "Lord, you orchestrated my days and my nights. You knew exactly what was going to become of that relationship and you protected me. I don't know why or how you did it; but I'm grateful that you did." I prayed out loud.

Since that day at the clinic, I had never told anyone about my close encounter with death or the bad news about Derron. My test was negative, so I felt no need to bother them with it. However, if my test had been positive, I would have confided in my family members only. But undoubtedly, I didn't want to put Derron on front-street like that with my friends, so I kept it to myself. If there was ever a need to tell someone about him, I vowed to myself, to the counselor at the health department counselor, and to my personal therapist that I would tell.

Vanessa and Belinda only thought I was going to see a therapist because I was depressed about my breakup, but I was really going because of the relationship, the test, and Derron's sexuality had really drained me physically and emotionally. I was emotionally bankrupt and needed to learn how to love myself again.

About five minutes later, Vanessa got back into the truck hyped as hell. "I can't wait to go the birthday bash! I'm going to get fucked up and fucked all at the same time!" I laughed and said, "Girl, your ass is crazy. Make sure you use condoms, alright." We jetted out to the house to get dressed because the Birthday Bash started at 9:30 pm. "We gotta hurry up get dress Nessa so we can get up in there." After we arrived at her house, we took turns showering and getting dressed, and then we hurried off to the Birthday Bash. At a quarter to ten we arrived at Gate B to enter the stadium where the stage was set up. Lil' John getting ready to perform and the crowd was going wild. I couldn't wait to get in, but we had arrived late and there were other people who were late getting there too. We waited patiently for the security guards to go through everyone's bag searching for weapons and other items, but it didn't bother us because we were both dancing in line to the music of the rappers on the loud speakers. "Damn, Seneca, we're next," Vanessa said putting out her cigarette. I took out the tickets to hand to the gatekeeper and as we were waiting to go through the gate he said, "Please step aside as for a minute." Vanessa and I looked at the each other with this "What tha fuck!" look. As we stepped aside, others were going through the gate one behind the other one. "Hey, you need to tell us what's going on. We're missing the show, man!" I exclaimed to the gatekeeper. He told another keeper to take his place at the gate; then he took us towards the front and told us that our tickets were counterfeit tickets and we wouldn't be able to go into the show. "What! Oh hell naw! I paid $50 dollars a piece for these tickets and I ain't about to go out like that! Uh… sir, you need to let us in cause we didn't know we were buying some fuck up tickets!" The keeper shook his head and asked Vanessa where she purchased the tickets. This time yelling and nearly crying Vanessa said, "On the streets by the Georgia Dome!" The keeper gave us a number to call to report the tickets and escorted us towards the exit. I was numb and stayed quiet for about 15 minutes while Vanessa almost blew a gasket in her head. I guess after all that I had been through nothing could move or shake me to the point of getting that angry. I allowed her to rant and rage for about 5 minutes then I told looked and there's nothing at all that we can do about it right this second. We missed out and lost money at the same time. The motherfucker who sold you the tickets got over on us, but that don't mean we have to let him fuck up our night. Then I suggested that we can go to the Ritz and that everything was on me. Vanessa settled down after about 30 minutes, and then when we got into the truck she drank a beer. We laughed at ourselves for getting messed up and headed to the club.

As usual the line was long so we waited a good 45 minutes to get inside the club. Inside, we made our way through the crowd to the restroom. In the restroom girls were smoking weed, dancing and talking to each other. There was also a stall-keeper in there selling candy, perfume, tampons and any other thing a female might need while being out in the club. "Girl, I'm so pissed off about those tickets that I need to hurry up and get me a drink!" Vanessa exclaimed. I quickly checked my makeup in the mirror and used the toilet. "Let's go Nessa," I said heading towards the bathroom exit. As soon as we opened the door niggas were standing around it trying to get our phone numbers and run game. Vanessa went to the bar, as I looked through the crowd, watching how the women were all up on the men and vice versa. I would have never thought that I would be back in a club after all I've been through. I felt someone tapping me on the shoulder but apparently I was daydreaming because it was Nessa. When she got my attention she said she had been calling my name for the longest time. "Girl, what's wrong with you? Are you alright?" she asked. I looked at her at and said, "Yeah, I'm fine. Come on let's walk around." We spotted an empty table and quickly ran over to sit at before someone else did. Once we sat down at the table Nessa said, "Umm... you did say everything was on you. Right?" I looked at her and laughed and told her to ahead and order because I had the tab. The waitress came over to take our order. "What will you ladies be having tonight?" she asked. I smiled at her and said, "I would like a Coke and a 20 piece hot wings with blue cheese and celery." Nessa then said, "Give me a Hennessey and Coke, one corona. I looked at her and batted my eyes and said, "Damn, I told you I was going to pay for your drinks and food, but don't get carried away!" The waitress laughed and walked off to fill our orders. We sat there listening to the music and then some guy came up to Nessa and asked her to dance. "Seneca, watch my pocketbook?" she said as she got up from the table. I nodded and kept listening to the music. As I sat there alone, I thought about my life and started wondering why I ever came to places like this. I looked over at Nessa and saw her dancing on the dance floor with this sexy Jamaican guy with dreads and I say to myself, "Well at least she's having a good time." Just then the waitress came back with our food and drinks. Nessa looked over and saw the waitress at the table and rushed over to get her drink. I reached into my pocketbook to get the money to pay for it, when the waitress informed me that a man in the VIP room had paid for my drinks and food and wanted me to join him there. "Oh hell… Yeah! That's what I'm talking about!" Nessa shouted. I looked at her smirking and then I shook my head. I asked the waitress who was he and she said that he was a regular who was a baller and had plenty of money. She told me he was wearing a Red Coogi shirt and a black hat with an "A" on it; then she walked away. "Vanessa, I'm not sure about meeting anyone right now. I just want to enjoy myself and go home by myself." As Vanessa lit up a cigarette she said, "Girl, don't compare everyone to that damn Derron! If this nigga want to wine and dine you … then let him! You'll never know, Sen. This could really be the one but you'll never know until you meet him. Look… if this motherfucker wants some pussy just because he paid for some hot wings and a couple of drinks he is going to be seriously disappointed!" I burst out laughing and told Vanessa she was a straight fool, and then I grabbed my jacket and purse and we walked through the club to the VIP room. The VIP room was in a class by itself and separated from the rest of the club. They kept it very dark in there, with only tea lights to pave the way to the high-backed chairs that sat back to back but in a circle of fours. The chairs were so big that they looked like they were made for kings and queens. I couldn't see in there, but once inside you could see out into the crowd. I didn't know what this guy looked like but I remembered the waitress telling me that he was wearing a red Coogi shirt and a black cap on with the letter "A" on it. We walked into the room and everyone was in their own little corners talking amongst themselves with their friends. As I looked to the left of the room I saw a very nice looking brown-skinned brother with a pointed nose and neatly trimmed mustache dressed in the description of clothing so we walked towards him. He smiled and gestured for us to sit down. "Hi, are you the guy who paid for our food and drinks?" I asked. He put his arms and in the air and said in a slurred voice, "Guilty," and then laughed. Vanessa then said, "Good, you are hereby sentenced to buying us more damn drinks!" He laughed out loud, and then he told the waiter in the VIP room to bring him two more beers. There were already five empty Corona bottles on the small table in front of him and I thought to myself that he must have had a party all by himself over here. We sat down and then he introduced himself as Keith. "Sweetheart, what's your name?" At first I was going to lie and make up a name, but I noticed that he was in fact very nice looking so I said, "Umm... my name is Seneca and this is Nessa." Nessa spoke and sat next to Keith and I sat across from him. Keith told me a little about himself and asked me some questions about myself. He told me that he was a contractor that built houses, and said that he was interested in getting to know me better. Nessa didn't have much to say at all she was just drinking, eating and listening to the music. In about two and a half hours tops, Keith must have gone through his entire bio because he had told me so much about himself, his family, career, friends and his cars. I started telling him about my kids and my career, and then I just happened to look at the time on my cellphone and noticed that it was 3:30 a.m in the morning. I looked over at Vanessa and she had fallen asleep. "Yeah, like I was saying, I..." but before I could complete my sentence, Keith suddenly interrupted me and said, "Seneca, Hold on I'll be right back. Man, I'm feeling a little sick on the stomach. Excuse me for a second I need to go the restroom." I asked him if he was going to be ok and before he could answer me he made a mad dash towards the door to go to the restroom with his hand over his mouth as if he was vomit. I notice that the VIP room was getting very quiet and people were starting leave. As I sat there waiting for Keith to return, I heard a guy with a deep voice talking and laughing with a lady. At first I did pay any attention to it and just continue listening to the music but then the started talking a little louder and his voice sounded kind of familiar. I also heard a girl talking but I couldn't make out her voice. "Who ever that guy is, he sure sounds familiar" I muttered as I looked over at

Nessa and she was still sleep. Then the guy said, "Yeah, that's some good shit." Immediately, my heart skipped beats and I felt a shortness of breath because that was a phrase the Derron use to say all the time. I needed to find out if that was him, but didn't want the guy to see me just in case it was him. I took out my mirrored makeup compact that had a small light on the inside of it to see if I could see who the guy was sitting on the other side. "Seneca, your mind is playing tricks on you," I kept telling myself. As the guy continued talking, my heartbeat became more rapid. "It just can't be. I just know that's not the man that I was in love with and who almost cost me my life," I repeated over and over to myself. Maybe this Keith slipped me a mickey in my drink and I'm hallucinating, I thought. I leaned over on the arm of the chair and flipped open the mirrored compact. As I positioned myself, I saw the back of a man's head with cornrow braids. I couldn't see his face, but every inch of my being strongly told me that it could be Derron. "Oh shit!" I said under my breath. My hand started trembling so much that the compact slipped out of hand and fell underneath the chair. I leaned over and tapped Nessa on the leg. "Vanessa, Vanessa, wake up," I whispered. She peeked out of one eye and said in a lethargic tone, "Wh-What is it?" I knelt down in front of the table and whispered to her that I believed that Derron was sitting on the other-side me talking to a girl." Vanessa looked at me in perplexity and said, "Ok, why don't you go speak to him?" I looked at her and said, "No! You don't understand. There's something I didn't tell you about Derron, but I have to tell you now." Vanessa saw that I was serious so she stucked her hand in the glass of water and splashed it on her face trying to sober herself up. Then she said in a nervous and inquisitive voice, "Tell me. Tell me … what's wrong?" I held up my finger gesturing to her to wait a second, and then I reached under the chair and picked up my mirrored compact. I got back into the chair and looked once more to see if he was still there. He was now sitting on the edge of the chair, so I saw the back of the shirt that he was wearing. It was a white T-shirt with a picture of Tupac on the back. Derron had one just like it that I'd bought him for his birthday. I quickly closed the compact and sighed, "That's him! That's him, Nessa! He's wearing the same Tupac shirt that I bought him!" She looked at me like I was crazy and said, "Girl, you sure ain't tripping. I thought you didn't drink alcohol. Do you know how many

Tupac shirts are out here in Atlanta?" she shook her head laughing. "You need to calm down Damn!" Vanessa cried. I put the compact in my purse and told Vanessa that I hadn't seen his face, but I was 99 percent sure that it was Derron. "So what Seneca, it's not like y'all are together or something. You can go where you want to go. He doesn't run you anymore, girl!" She said in smart ass tone. As I grabbed my jacket, I told Vanessa that he was HIV positive and that I believe that he knows that I know about it because the Health Department called me to come gets tested and he gave her my name as well as other girls." Vanessa took a hard swallow and looked down at the plate with the blue cheese dip on it that she and I had shared and said, "D-Do you have it?" I grabbed her hand and said tentatively, "No girl, I don't! I'll explain everything else to you later, but right now we have to get the hell out of here!" Vanessa became very bemused and whispered, "Wait, Wait. Seneca, but you have got to tell that girl he is talking to about him, if that's him. You just have too!" looked at her with doubt on my face and said, "I know but I'mm... let's just go!" I remembered the promise I made to the counselor and and my therapist that I would tell if there was a needed to and this was one of those "**NEED TO**" moments. Just when we was getting ready to get up, the DJ started playing the country music that informed everyone that the club was getting ready to close. We knew that after the played that country music; we would only had seconds before the lights in the whole club came on. Vanessa jumped up from her seat and swiftly walked out of the VIP room, leaving me behind Like she was the cowardly lion in the, Wizard of Oz. I covered my face with my hand as I swiftly walked towards the door; when I realized that Vanessa had ran out and left her purse on the floor. "Damn!" I said and quickly turned around to go get it. As I stooped down to get her purse that was stuck underneath the table's leg, I heard him say tell to the girl that she could stay just spent the night with me. I was nervous as ever and I finally got her purse detached from the leg of the table. As I raised my head, I saw the girl standing up and putting her jacket on. I could only hear my heartbeat as things seemed to have been moving in slow motion now. Just as I stood up with Vanessa's purse in my hand to make a mad dash for the door again, the lights flicked on in the club and the guy had gotten out of the claim. He turned around about the same time as I was trying to make it to the door. When he turned around our eyes met each other. It was Derron looking skinner than I remembered my worst nightmare had revisited me and was staring me right in my face. I dropped the purses and my jacket and stood there frozen just like I had just seen a ghost. As I looked at him a tear fell down my cheek and I could hear the girl asking, "What's was wrong and why is that bitch staring at?" When the lights came on Vanessa came back to the entrance of the VIP room and I could also hear her belligerently yelling, "Go head and tell her! Goddamn it, call that fucking nigga' out!" I was caught inside of a zone between love, fear, hurt and unresolved anger and the only person I could see was Derron everything else around me sounded like echoes in a hollow cave. Derron looked cold and I could see straight through his dysfunctional soul. I strongly felt that he was aware that he was HIV positive and that he was about make this girl a victim of his venom and take away her option to live. His soul looked at me through his morosed eyes as if they were silently begging me to walk away and not to say a word.

TELLS FROM THE HEART
YOU PUSHED ME

You pushed me into my destiney. You gave me heartache and pain and bad memories is all I ever had to gain. Yes, it was you pushed to see myself in a different light; gave me to power to let go of a relationship that wasn't quite, right. It was you who pushed me, when I wanted to cling on, because I was so afraid of being alone.

You actually helped me to understand the meaning of that damn love song, "It takes a fool to learn that love don't love no body." And a fool I once was… your damn fool and with all the power you thought you had over me, had I never went through this shit you would still be dragging me!

Yes, it was you who pushed me.

Thanks for that push. What once was a heart of mush is now a heart tougher than stone. The only different is; it knows how to let go when someone claims to love… and still do wrong?

Stronger than ever, got my shit together. Looking forward to another day; got thru it because I prayed.

So it true, return good for the evil that people do to you. So when you read this, they can take it to the heart.

Cause had it not been for you pushing me, I wouldn't have received such a great award.

YOU PUSHED ME!

CHOOSE TO LOVE

If you choose not to love me, that would be ok. I choose to love you in everyway.

You see, loving you takes much more effort; more than I'm able to give.

I love you, I'm loving you with my own free will.

No matter what you have, what you look like or what you give. When there is nothing left; my love will manifest and be revealed.

The kind of love I possess for you is thicker than skin,

but in your heart you have built up a wall and won't allow me to come in.

I would even go as far to as say that I have love for your mother, Although, I never met her because she gave birth to you. And although, God has called her home, when I see the hurt thru your soul, I know that she will always be will.

Loving you is loving everything you stand for and hope for; whether it good or bad and assuring you that I will be there to wipe away your tears, when you are sad.

Because whether you realize it or not; you are so much more than you allow to appear. You are deep in thought, firm on the surface, yet very sincere.

So, I choose to love you, even if you decide not to love me back. But just be mindful that a soulmate never came in the form of a Cadillac.

YOU AIN'T NOTHING BUT A SNAKE

Nigga, you ain't nothing but a snake! And that game of yours is so fucking tired that you need to retire, your old 900 block of Glynn Oak street, doing the two-steps in the young folks club. Riding around on some rent and roll dubs?

Faking like a real playa, when you don't have two nickels to rub together to make a dime.
Oh, did I say dime?

Yeah, that dime bag of weed and two, fifty-cents blunt. Nigga, you really thought you were a stunt!

I made holidays special and gave you a birthday cake; then you turn around a bite and said,

Bitch, you knew I was a snake!

Hiding behind your seventeen braids and your black, uncircumcised dick; gave you're the notion that you can have any fucking chick.

You rode around in your caddy and kept gum to freshen your breath. Good front, but not good enough because I love you more than you love your damn self!

Womanizer, Satan deskieser, but you are still on the down-low. I should have looked before I leaped, because all the friends thought you were slow.

So go ahead you wangster, keep having your fun. But you will always be the jack of all trades, yet a master of none!